Not The Fainting Kind

Not That Kind Of Dandy 2

Will Soulsby-McCreath

ISBN: 978-1-917179-00-3 (paperback), 978-1-917179-01-0 (eBook)
First Edition

WillSoulsbyMcCreath.com

For those of us who never seem to be enough.

I have shared a bonus short story, *Not The Ignorant Kind* at the end of this book. It's Tao's perspective about the mystery Nat presents to him and is a great recap of the previous novel for those who may want or need it.

And, in keeping with the format of *Not The Fighting Kind*, I have also included one of the later chapters from Tao's perspective too: *Not The Wanting Kind*.

A quick note about pronouns:

If you are unfamiliar with neo-pronouns, they do appear in this novel. In particular you'll come across the singular they, as well as others like ey, eir, em and xe, xyr, xem.

Also By Will Soulsby-McCreath

The Guardian Cadet Series
Merry Arlan: Breaking The Curse
Merry Arlan: Finding The Heir
Kitty Hughes: An Unexpected Meeting (short story)

Welcome To Humanity

Inter-Planetary Alliance Novels
Unlicensed Delivery

Not That Kind Of Dandy
Not The Fighting Kind
Not The Fainting Kind
Not That Kind Of Dandy Omnibus

Not The Fainting Kind

Not That Kind Of Dandy

2

Will Soulsby-McCreath

Prologue
I Won't Even Need A Sword

"Darling, Peaches, Sweet Pea." With each pretty nickname, the elegantly dressed pirate approached. The high winds tousled the bright red curls bouncing across their head, away from their sharp featured face. "I'm not sure what you've heard about dandies. I imagine you think dandies weak. And I certainly am the quintessential dandy."

They held no weapons, hands open as if ready to catch something out of thin air. Their shirt sleeves clung to their arms, too tight to logically allow for freedom of movement. The dynamic peacock patterned waistcoat hugged their torso, shining silk shifting with each breath. It shouldn't have made a threatening image.

Their face darkened. "But you could not pry this ship from my cold, dead hands."

The naval officer snorted, nostrils flaring with the noise. A Commodore, by the epaulettes on his uniform. The faded blue and dirtied white of his jacket sat a little ill, as if he had been at sea too long and some of his bulk had abandoned him.

"Just look at your crew." The dandy pirate gestured, stepping closer to the Commodore while he was distracted. Their nose wrinkled at the scent washing off him: perfume over the odour of an unwashed body. A smell too often found on naval officers. His brown hair stuck to his head with the grease of too long without a wash. "They're trying so desperately to subdue mine, but it won't work. Do you see?"

Below the pair of commanding officers, on the main deck of the pirate ship, clean and well-dressed pirates clashed in a chaotic maelstrom with dirty naval officers in ill-fitting too-worn uniforms.

"Fear," the Dandy Pirate Captain whispered into the Commodore's ear. "Fear for what my crew could do when they fail. Fear for what you will subject them to if they live through that failure."

The Commodore's head snapped toward the dandy.

It made a certain level of twisted, naval sense that he had sought out the captain of the vessel. As if life ever made that kind of match. As if pirates worked like that. He probably just wanted the challenge of the strongest pirate available. Poor choice on his part. He'd have had more fun fighting Bear or Aleksei.

Still, the Dandy Pirate Captain lifted his face with delicate fingers on his chin, forcing him to meet their hard eyes. "That's the big difference between you and me, Peaches—apart from your generally unwashed state. I cultivated my crew. I provide for their every need. And *I* was democratically voted in."

They smiled and stepped back. "But I know you're unlikely to be convinced by my simple words." They swung their arms wide, half invitation, half mockery of a bow. "Take your best shot. I won't even need a sword to defeat you."

1

I Will Bring You To Your Knees

There was something particular about partnered dancing, which quartet or larger-group dancing managed to avoid. If one misjudged one's lead in a quartet or larger, it was easy to recover, for one's partner and for the quartet itself. The vast majority of the time, in a quartet or larger, mistakes became unnoticeable. With partnered dancing, however, a single wrong step had one careening into their partner. Most of the time that resulted in disaster. One particularly memorable case had included knocking a partner clear to the ground.

These days, Nat would be more likely to compare a quartet or larger to being like a well bonded ship's crew. Everyone moving in unison, clear on their own steps, and ready to step in to cover for one another's occasional missteps.

Nat's current position, however, was far more like partnered dancing. Facing someone one-on-one. Worse still, Nat definitely didn't know the steps and, certainly, should not have accepted the dance. Or egged on the Naval Commodore in question with a comment so boastful as not needing a sword of their own to defeat him.

The Commodore's sword rasped from its scabbard. The click of his heels meeting carried over the swoosh of the waves and the quieting sounds of the fight below.

Nat's heart demanded their attention, thumping heavily in their chest. What had they been thinking inviting him to fight? No. They knew what they had been thinking. That maybe, just maybe, their absurd over-confidence would be enough to put him off fighting all together.

Still. Such was the situation they found themself in.

Nat didn't even own a sword.

The Commodore thrust his sword toward them. Nat sidestepped the blade, feet moving in steps more practised in a very different scenario. The Commodore's feet, set shoulder width apart, moved. The front one stepping, the back one filling the gap.

"Are you seriously trying to fence with me? You can't fence a weaponless opponent, Peaches." Not to mention that wasn't a fencing sword. Who promoted this guy?

"You will not pick up a weapon with which to defend yourself," the Commodore snarled.

Nat presented their practised dandified smile. All ease and a little bit of snark. "I told you, I don't need one."

The next sword swipe held more aggression. With aggression came speed, leaving Nat reeling away from haphazard swings. The edge of the ship rapidly approached. Did he intend to push Nat overboard? As if any pirate captain worth their title wouldn't know ever millimetre of their ship with their eyes closed?

The blade glinted in the sun. Nat's eyes stung with the light. They swung an arm up to block their face. A burn of pain slashed across their forearm. Shit. The blade had caught them.

Still blinking away sunspots, Nat squinted as the Commodore whipped the blade at them once again. It came down as if to cleave their arm from their shoulder.

A tiny "Eep" escaped Nat, completely without their permission. They dashed to one side.

The sword lodged in the stern of the ship.

The Commodore yanked it. It didn't budge. He drew a dagger from his belt.

Nat didn't quite dodge fast enough. The blade cut into their waistcoat fabric, clanging against the boning that sat under the line of buttons down the front. It bounced out, bringing frayed silk with it.

"I will remove you from that high horse, deviant!" the Commodore snarled. "I will drag you to your knees."

They always seemed to think words like 'deviant' would hurt Nat's feelings. Always dove for them in the wake of a gentle prod like Peaches. Nat had heard worse. Nat had claimed worse.

On the Commodore's next jab, Nat spun around him, a move entirely drawn out of the popular dances from the last time they had been present in high society and been forced into dancing even though they never wanted to. They grabbed the man's shoulder and yanked his torso down into their rising knee. That wasn't part of the dance.

The wind rushed from the Commodore's lungs. The knife in his hand clattered to the wooden floor beneath them, skittering down the stairs to be lost in the chaos on the main deck.

Continuing their momentum, Nat grabbed the Commodore's wrist and yanked it behind his back. They whipped off the man's cravat —really? A simple slip knot?— and wrapped the fabric around the captured wrist.

They slammed their knee into his ribs again, further winding him so they could grab the other hand and secure it in the cravat-ropes. A harsh hand on his shoulders, they shoved him down onto the deck, whispering delicately into his ear, "What was that about knees?"

The Commodore struggled in his restraints, trying to at least drive to his feet. A broad hand clamped down on his shoulder, pinning him to the deck.

Nat smiled up at Bear. "You've corralled his men already, I take it?"

Bear nodded, pride fluttering over him as clearly as his neatly tied cravat strings. At least there was someone around who could tie a decent cravat.

"Well, Peaches," they said to the Commodore. "If you're a good boy, we can all come out the other side of this alive."

The Commodore's eyes gleamed, eyebrows drawn low over them. His jaw stood out starkly under the at-sea beard. Did nobody have any pride in their appearance anymore?

"Bear, if you wouldn't mind escorting him back to his ship?"

Once he was over the plank and back on his ship —speed encouraged by a few gentle pokes of a sword from Jay— Kajal the rigger and Nat shoved the boarding plank into the sea, stirring up white foam.

Nat blew a kiss over the gap between the vessels as *Mercy's Myth* began to sail away from the gutted naval ship. The clean white sails billowed in the wind like jellyfish tentacles in a strong current, cut to ribbons by Nat's crew.

The gold handle of the sword now lodged in the ship glittered in the early morning light. The gilt wire knot swinging lightly with the motion of the ship. It had cleaved straight into one of the last vestiges of the previous Captain's reign: a mostly worn away carving of the ship's original name. One of many changes Nat had implemented upon being voted in as Captain. Alongside the insistence that everybody go out and buy themselves new clothes with no obvious damage.

After all, Nat's first task upon boarding had been to repair the endless stacks of damaged, aged clothing that the crew had been offered as their only possible attire. It wasn't that, as Captain, Nat had any real issue helping to mend crew's clothing if needed, but that pile of broken clothes had been the first thing to go. Why set themself the endless task when there was plenty of money available to just buy new clothes. Especially ones that helped the crew feel comfortable in their own bodies.

With a final glance at the sword, Nat slipped away from the main deck and into the captain's cabin, closing the door behind them and leaning their head against the wood.

In the almost-year that Nat had been freely aboard, they liked to linger on the deck, interacting with the crew, moving around the ship that had once been their prison, proving themself useful. But that interaction had been way too close to taking Nat out. They should have known better, should have done better. Aleksei was always telling them to hide if they ever got boarded. Nat had all but promised to do so. But when it had actually happened, they'd frozen. All too caught up in the last time they had been on a ship that got boarded.

The knock reverberated through them, yanking them all too brutally out of that memory.

Nat surged away from the door, trying to pretend they were looking at something on the huge desk that took up most of the space in the captain's cabin. Sadly, they'd actually tidied away all the papers so that ruse fell apart before it began.

Thankfully, Aleksei was too wrapped up in what had brought him into the cabin in the first place. His pale eyebrows tugged low over his stunningly golden eyes. "You need to be more careful."

"It's all about the destruction of their confidence," Nat argued. They didn't want to seem weak. They couldn't afford it. They brushed hands down the front of their waistcoat, grimacing when they came across the damage, poking at the similar hole in their shirt sleeve. "At least I wasn't wearing the jacket," they mourned.

Aleksei opened his mouth, sighed, and closed it. He folded his arms, covering his partially exposed chest where he hadn't bothered buttoning his shirt. For all that their frames matched one another; Aleksei was the antithesis of Bear when it came to clothes. Aleksei was a little shorter, a little narrower in the shoulder, but it hardly made much of a difference. He, like Bear, was a giant specimen of a person. They had made quite the impression, each stood behind their particularly short previous captain with her ridiculously sized hat. Especially since, back then, they'd been in a similar state of undress, Bear unable to wear a shirt with the way it pressed against the damage done to his throat in some long ago and unforgettable past.

If Nat hadn't met a pirate like Tao, they might have started thinking all pirates —bar said ex-captain— were bulky like Aleksei and Bear. Everyone on the ship was corded with muscles. But Tao's frame was so much like Nat's own. In the comfortable ranges between average heights for various genders —in Tao's case, short for a man— and slim built. In their year of relative freedom aboard the ship, Nat had yet to meet another pirate shaped like Tao. Or themself.

"I've asked Hui to take us to the nearest Pirate Port to trade the loot anyway," Aleksei said, finally finding his words. "You can replace or repair it there."

"That would be..." Think of them and they shall appear. "Tao?"

Nat was still learning a lot about navigating the seas, and the exact location of the Pirate Ports were a closely guarded secret. Even to pirate captains, or at least pirate captains like Nat. They unbuttoned their shirt cuff and rolled up their sleeve to check the wound beneath. A small scratch, it wasn't even bleeding. "We'll have to come up with a gift for tribute. But I suppose there are no other options when the navy besieges you without warning."

"Do they ever give warning?"

Not in Nat's experience. Their hand crept to the line of scars decorating their left arm. Nobody did.

Aleksei cleared his throat, looking away from Nat's reminder of the injury he had been party to. Another gift from the previous captain. "I'm sure you regaling Lord Tao with tales of taking down a naval officer with nothing but his neck cravat might appease."

Nat didn't think about their experiences with Tao and cravats. They definitely didn't think of the feeling of Tao sliding the fabric from around their neck and using it to bind their hands the same way they had done with the naval officer. Except Tao and Nat hadn't been in a fight when he had done it, they had been in a bed. The fight part had come later...

"It's just a cravat, Lyosha, not a neck cravat."

Aleksei said nothing.

Nat sighed. If Aleksei had already set in the course there was little they could do to change it. At least not without a reason the crew would agree to. And they'd been holding off returning to Shenai for long enough. It would start looking suspicious soon. "How long until we arrive?"

"Less than an hour."

"I should change into an uninjured outfit. See if you can get that blade out of the ship when you have the time?" The fewer reminders about the navy around them the better.

2
Quite The Unorthodox Tribute

Tao sat astride his throne —it could only be titled as such in the same way his palace could never merely be called a mansion. The pagoda style building with its gold-tipped red rooves and huge white stone wall surrounding the grounds was both akin to the mansions Nat had grown up visiting and, at the same time, completely set apart from them. Not just in style but in sheer size. It screamed palace, particularly surrounded by the smaller and more humble village in the valley below that opened into the sea.

One of Tao's legs lay over the arm of the throne, cushioned in green fabric, the other foot flat on the floor, giving the impression of decadence, relaxation, and even the theoretical invitation to more intimate activities. A carefully chosen pose.

Nat steeled themself and stepped up to offer their tribute. Their shoes clacked noisily against the tiled floor. Naval boots liked to announce themselves. The throne room sprawled out around them, just as decadent as the Pirate Lord himself. Despite being clad in the same greens and golds as this throne, Tao was always the first thing to draw the eye. His wide, dark eyes, easily smiling face, and charming words could steal one's very self out from under them and convince them they'd given it freely. The ultimate, quintessential pirate. And a dandy to boot.

Nat retracted their hands, as he took the tribute from them. They stepped away from the throne, desperate for as much distance as possible between themself and the Pirate Lord. They tugged one sleeve cuff then the other, as if either needed to be set right. The shirt itself —chosen to match the colour scheme of Tao's palace— was pastel green and paired particularly nicely with the flashy bronze waistcoat Nat would never have got away with in high society, particularly not when paired with the technically-matching brown trousers. They hadn't bothered with a jacket. Not in the unrelenting heat of Shenai. Even without it, Nat's skin had beaded with sweat on the walk up from the docks.

"Captain Nat." Tao pursed his lips, flipping through the leather wrapped, handwritten manuscript Nat had handed over. "This is quite the unorthodox tribute."

It was only a few pages, hardly requiring leather wrapping but Nat had needed it to look nice. "I asked Hui to translate it for you."

"Hui?"

"My navigator."

"Most people call that a Boatswain."

"Do they." It wasn't a question.

Tao's dark eyes flicked up to Nat. "Adding Un-Coded crew members? Careful, Captain, or you'll sway your ratios too far and might be barred access to Pirate Ports altogether."

"As far as I understood it, the first step would be losing out on privileges, not being barred completely."

"Not that it isn't an... interesting tribute," Tao said. "But there is something else I had in mind."

Nat pressed their tongue against their teeth, the sharp edge digging into soft flesh. "Do tell."

"Information." He shifted his feet to the floor.

Nat swallowed. *Don't come any closer. Please don't.* "What kind of information might you be seeking?"

"I came across this piece of postage."

"Is that so?"

"Addressed to someone I'm not sure if I know."

What game was he playing? Even so, Nat couldn't deny the invitation. They had always been bad at saying no and worse at saying no to Pirate Lord Tao. "Do tell. Perhaps I can offer a little clarity."

"Liege." He paused long enough for Nat's heart to ricochet around their chest.

Liege. Tao was one of the few who knew beyond a shadow of a doubt that Liege had been Nat's title before landing themself upon a boat.

"N." Again that pause. As if allowing Nat the time to recognise that their own name began with N. As if they needed it. Or maybe just to allow the final piece of information to hit with the utmost impact.

"Adelhard."

The floor fell away under Nat's feet, leaving them awash in the sea of roiling emotions.

Adelhard.

Fuck.

How had he found that? How did he know? How had he partnered it up with Nat? By what means had this particular piece of post appeared in Shenai Pirate Port of all places? And, possibly more importantly, who had sent it? Who would be sending any attempts at contact to Liege N. Adelhard at sea? Had it been sent before Nat had been brought aboard a pirate ship? Or had it been sent after their official disappearance?

They cleared their throat, knowing by the way Tao's eyes clung to them that they had been quiet too long. They smoothed hands down their waistcoat. "My Lord?"

He pulled a folded rectangle of paper from a hidden compartment in his throne. In another circumstance Nat might have teased about Tao and his secrets. Secret doors, secret compartments, traditional secrets. But, in the wake of that family name, Nat wasn't in much of a teasing mood.

"I have here." He twisted the letter between his fingers, creating illusions as the front flicked between red wax and black ink address. The last time Nat had seen a letter like that they had likened it to an execution order. Somehow this felt no different. "A letter addressed to one Liege N. Adelhard. And I thought to myself, who might know where Liege N. Adelhard would be found?"

Nat's attention clung to the letter as Tao shifted to his feet. As he approached them.

"And then I thought about the only Liege I knew. The Liege-turned-Captain. Un-Coded Captain on a Coded Ship. Dandy of the high seas." With each pause he took another singular step forward, an elegant and dangerous dance.

Nat's heart thundered so hard in their chest it might well have been Felitabby trying to escape, those last few days of his life spent trapped in the same cells as Nat in the bowels of the ship that was now titled *Mercy's Myth*. He had been held for ransom too.

"Captain Nat," Tao continued, "with the fashion sense most couldn't contemplate while living on a ship. Captain Nat, ex-prisoner turned mutineer." He leaned closer to whisper in Nat's ear, sending a shudder over them, "Captain Nat, who once told me I wasn't the only one with a title. Captain Nat, the self-proclaimed unransomable."

Nat closed their eyes, took a deep breath, desperate to steel themself to the task at hand. They had managed it for so long, kept everything about their history secret from the people in their life now. And, just like that, it was shattered. They were, once again, an Adelhard. And they would have to cope with whatever that meant from this point onward.

They opened their eyes and held out a hand. He knew anyway. He wasn't asking. Just because he phrased it as questions didn't mean anything. This was dandy information sharing. The questions weren't the point. The point was the reaction to them and Nat had been foolishly unguarded, unfortunately unprepared for a revelation such as this. There were few courses of action open to them.

"We both know what you know, Tao. Can I have my letter or not?"

A silent, breathless moment passed. Tao pressed the paper into Nat's waiting palm. Nat's fingers clamped tightly around it. They itched to open it, to search through for any information it might contain. But not yet. Not in front of Tao. Not in front of Tao in the mood he presented.

"Oh, Dandy," he sighed, breath ghosting over Nat's neck.

They swallowed thickly. Interactions with Tao ever since that fight had been fraught. Impossible. Filled with an immeasurable amount of emotions that all combined as strong and relentless as the storm that had driven them together to begin with.

The warmth of Tao's body seeped into Nat's front, his neck was exposed and so close to their lips. So easy to turn this tension into a different kind. So easy to use the information they had learnt in their brief, unforgettable and ill-advised intimacies. But Nat wasn't about to start using intimacy like that, as a weapon or a tool. And the letter addressed to their old life weighed heavy in their hand.

"If there is nothing else," they said. It came out a whisper. "I must find a tailor in your port."

Tao leaned back, still close enough for his breath to brush against Nat's face in a gentle caress. He raised an eyebrow.

"An altercation with the navy that didn't go as smoothly as I might have liked."

"Do tell," he invited.

Nat's lips shifted into that easy, practised, dandy smile. "Perhaps another time."

"Is that a promise?"

$\mathcal{N}$at slumped into the chair behind their desk back on *Mercy's Myth*. They dropped the letter on the table top, warring between the urgent need to open it and the overwhelming dread of what might be contained within.

Upon leaving Tao's palace, in the relative seclusion of the trees and bushes that surrounded the outer wall, but before they headed back to the port, Nat had shoved the letter underneath their waistcoat. Flinching every time the paper crackled against their shirt, half-convinced everyone around them could hear it. Paranoia spurring them into faster motion.

That it had ended up in Tao's hands, the pirate who had the best chance of figuring out the connection between Liege Adelhard and Nat was almost unthinkable. Nat had imagined all sorts of ways their crew might discover their family name, but Tao had never been part of that equation. After their initial flirtation, even with Tao having quite literally handing Nat back to the captain who kept them as prisoner for ransom, Nat had seen a safety in Tao.

He was a dandy, they had thought that meant he wouldn't sell them out, that he might keep information like this quiet. But the way he had presented the letter, the way he had sighed that *"Dandy"* onto Nat's neck, disappointed and still holding that same intrigue that had summoned Nat into his bed in the first place. He wasn't just a dandy, Tao was a Pirate Lord and Nat couldn't yet know what that might mean for their secrets. The information Nat had gathered so far only indicated that they were bad at talking to Pirate Lords. Nat had alienated at least two already, the third treated Aleksei more like the captain than Nat, and then there was Tao...

Nat dropped their head into their hands. "What am I going to do?"

"What?" Aleksei's head poked around the open doorway.

"Nothing, never mind." They yanked the letter down into their lap.

Aleksei stepped into the captain's cabin, shutting the door behind him. "What's wrong?"

"I just said it was nothing."

"No, you said 'nothing, never mind,' which is Nat for 'there is something I want to talk about but I feel like I can't,' which means a closed door conversation."

"You're annoying."

"Because I'm right." He perched on the edge of Nat's desk. "Is it Tao?"

"In a way."

"Tao is one of the Pirate Lords—"

"I know, I know," Nat cut in. "Pirate Lords, Pirate Ports, Pirate Code. Discounts, protection, and so on."

Aleksei had first mentioned the Code and the Pirate Queen to whom all Coded Pirates swore their allegiance when Nat had been a prisoner set for ransom on this very ship. He had expanded further when Nat had been voted in as captain, but never quite got through one whole explanation, always feeding Nat dribs and drabs of information. Little pieces they had to puzzle together for themself.

It wasn't intentional; he was just very situational about it. Giving Nat what they needed most immediately. And, after a few months, and having been introduced to one of the four Pirate Lords officially as Captain of *Mercy's Myth*, it seemed like Aleksei had forgotten that Nat hadn't been introduced to the pirate way of life by choice. That people had kept things from them intentionally as part of their imprisonment.

The soft smile on Aleksei's face as the sunlight filtered through the wavy windows at the back of the cabin softened the edges of Nat's mood. They leaned their head on their hands, elbows on the desk. "It's not his Pirate Lord status that's the problem."

The problem was that Nat's fickle heart was proving to be a little more steadfast than they had anticipated. The problem was that Nat had thought returning to Shenai, triumphantly a pirate Captain and dressed in appropriate attire would put them on similar footing, would balance the awkward power dynamic between the two. Would finally answer the questions Tao had fired at them.

But it seemed Tao hadn't liked it. Hadn't liked them as their true self. Only liked them as someone to be rescued.

And none of that even touched on what Nat might find in the letter. The letter that Tao knew about. The letter that informed him of Nat's most closely guarded secret: their family name.

And if he shared that, who was to say the crew of *Mercy's Myth* wouldn't try what they had intended with Nat in the very beginning and attempt to ransom them back to their family? What would be stopping them?

3
The Voice Of Davy Jones Himself

A knock had both Nat and Aleksei turning to face the door. "Come in?"

"A request from the Pirate Lord." Nafia held the paper between two fingers, giving it as little contact as humanly possible. She strode over to Nat's desk and dropped it unceremoniously on the red leather top.

"It's not going to bite you, Nafia."

"I would rather stay as far away from the Pirate Lord and anything he has ever touched as possible, thank you."

Nat and Aleksei shared a sidelong glance. If that were truly the case, Nafia wouldn't want to be anywhere near either of them.

"See!" Nafia cried. "I knew it. I knew there was something about him and you and —"

"Nafia," Nat interrupted. "It's nothing important."

The surgeon folded her arms.

"Just because you're asexual doesn't mean we all have to be."

Nafia scrunched her nose in a playful scowl. "Don't be gross."

"That's not what this is anyway," Nat called after her as she left.

The card itself was a simple piece of paper, folded neatly in half. No seals of complex addresses, not even a name on the outside. Tall, thin, evenly spaced letters requested Nat join the Pirate Lord for dinner.

Dinner with Tao... Nat tried to push aside thoughts of the last time they had shared a meal with him.

Phantom pain washed over Nat's scarred left arm. Without thought they rubbed at the neat lines carved into their skin beneath their shirt sleeve.

Aleksei's eyes fixed on the motion.

Tao had offered Nat so much when they had so little. But when they had something, some level of power, some piece of control, he hadn't wanted them anymore.

"What does the card say?" Aleksei asked, voice hoarse.

"An invitation to dinner."

Aleksei's mouth settled into a firm line.

Nat frowned. "Does that mean something to you that it doesn't to me?"

"Not necessarily." It sounded like a question.

Nat waited.

As usual, Aleksei broke easily, words spilling out of his mouth. "But, I have never known Tao to invite someone to dinner publicly unless he intends to use that as leverage for something else."

The paper in Nat's lap weighed heavy again. They knew what he wanted. But what could they do? They had been publicly invited to dinner with the Pirate Lord. A good, Coded captain would go. Wouldn't they?

*N*at rolled their shoulders back before stepping through the huge doors into Tao's throne room. This evening wasn't going to be easy. Made all the more difficult by Aleksei's insistence on strategizing all afternoon.

He'd grilled Nat on everything with only the exception of table manners, thankfully not so wrapped up in his paranoia as to forget that Nat had been instructed in proper table manners from childhood. His words swam around in Nat's head for the entire walk up the hill to Tao's palace. Questioning what the Pirate Lord might want. Theorising about the ways he might try to convince Nat to give up information. Tellingly, Aleksei had fumbled over his words with one of the possibilities, glancing at Nat's bed tucked away in a corner of the captain's cabin. Fooled into thinking Nat wouldn't be able to extrapolate his intended meaning. He was worried Tao would try to do exactly what the ship's previous captain had set Aleksei to the task of. Using intimacy to break down Nat's defences.

He wouldn't. Nat knew him better than that. Like Nat, Tao believed there was no value in an intimacy shared without full and clear consent.

In the large, marble room, the throne itself sat empty.

Nat froze, mid-step. Their eyes flicked around the room to see if Tao was hiding somewhere to surprise them. The cream coloured walls were empty, no extra shadows lingering around the throne itself. Where exactly would one hide in an empty, open room anyway?

In the silence, the chirping and whirring of evening bugs from outside found its way through the windows along with the cool evening breeze.

Nat approached the throne, stepping only on their toes to prevent their heels clicking against the tile. They'd only seen it empty once and it hadn't exactly been a focal point back then. Nat had been too fixated on the captain who had taken them hostage as she bartered for their return to her.

It was a massive wooden thing with cushions and drapery so carefully placed atop it. And a little rectangle of creamy white paper in the seat. Keeping their attention half on their surroundings, primed for the opening of a secret door, Nat lifted the paper.

Dearest Captain, it would please me if you followed the cards. T.

The same neat, tall script as the invitation to dinner.

Nat didn't crumple the paper, but the urge to do so made the muscles in their arm tense. They drew in a deep breath.

Each Pirate Lord had their own way of running their domains. The Pirate Lord of the Frozen Wastes ran regular banquets for visiting captains. The tribute was each Captain's time, though she had spent far more time talking with Aleksei than Nat. The Pirate Lord of the Equatian Islands only accepted luxury items: jewels, fine fabrics, and the like. She had literally requested the jacket off Nat's back upon their introduction. The Pirate Lord of the Dry Sea expected spices or interesting regional items. Xe had a hankering for Aleksei's sword, a rare Kovian design xe said. Once they'd got back to the ship, Aleksei had explained that his father had made the sword before Aleksei had taken to the seas. That was how Nat had ended up in an argument with their third Pirate Lord.

And then there was Tao, Pirate Lord of Shenai. The first Pirate Lord Nat had ever met, the first with whom they had argued, and the last to get their official introduction of captaincy. He asked for something the Captain considered valuable, it turned out.

Nat placed his note into the pocket of their delicate green and gold paisley jacket. They shifted around the throne room to the huge doors behind it. The only visible doors in the throne room that didn't lead back out the exit. Nat had been through those doors once, in the opposite direction.

If Nat remembered the route to Tao's hideaway room, they could have forgone the search for notes, but they had thought they wouldn't need to retrace those steps so they hadn't bothered to pay attention.

The corridor stretched out in front of them, all dark woods, deep greens, and gold decorations. Nat trailed a hand over the intricate gold carvings decorating one wall. Tao's taste stood out across the entire building. Surprising, considering he had apparently taken it over from the previous Pirate Lord of Shenai.

They pulled their hand away as they recognised the suggestive nature of the shadows being played out on the wall behind the carving.

A note tucked slightly under the carpet runner simply read, '*You missed one, T.*' Forcing Nat to trek half way back to the throne room to find the missing note.

Each short, cryptic message led Nat further through Tao's palace until finally they emerged into his secluded receiving room. The same room as last time. It hadn't changed. Two green velvet sofas faced one another over a squat, dark wood table. Gold and clear glass lanterns cast their soft glow over the room, over Tao and his shining dark hair. It cascaded around his shoulders instead of its usual plait.

He lounged on one of the sofas, facing away from the door through which Nat entered. "I see you managed my little puzzle."

Nat shifted around the sofas to see the smug look on his face, pointedly avoiding the section of wall that they knew hid a door to the secret bedroom.

"It wasn't particularly challenging, My Lord," they lied. Some of those notes had been so well hidden that Nat was sure they hadn't got them all. Just like they were sure Tao recognised the words for the lie they were.

"Please sit." Tao gestured to the seat opposite him. It was all so reminiscent of that first meeting; Nat almost couldn't bring themself to do it.

The shoof of a door opening behind Nat brought their hand to the back of their neck, as if it would stop the sensation of crawling bugs as one of Tao's people set a tray of tea things on the squat table and disappeared through a different door.

Under their hair, Nat glanced at the hidden door to the bedroom, cheeks heating with the memory. *'Be a good Dandy and keep your hands there for me.'*

"Tea?" Tao offered, serving Nat a cup.

They took the delicate porcelain in hand. A Shenai style cup with no handle, but Nat had drunk tea out of tankards at this point. The swirling scent of jasmine scented steam filled the room. There really was nothing like it.

"How long has it been since you last sat to have proper tea?" Tao's soft voice shrouded Nat like steam.

"Too long," they admitted without thinking.

"Ever since you left your family home?"

Nat glared. "The last time I sat to have proper tea was in this very room with you a year ago." Give or take.

"Not when you left high society, then?"

"I knew that was why you called me here."

"Can you blame me?"

Nat set the tea cup down on the table. It thunked lightly on the surface. A rumble of thunder for the impending storm. "For what, exactly?"

"For my interest. Don't let me stop you enjoying your tea."

Nat didn't say that holding a steaming cup of tea while Tao followed this line of enquiry would lead to the risk of Tao getting tea tossed in his face. "If I finish that tea, your people will bring the next course on your carefully worded statement. If I must walk out, I would like to retain the dignity of doing it over tea rather than a meal."

Tao's facade faded. He sat up, setting his own tea cup on the table next to Nat's, the light reflected off the shifting liquid. A flash of lightning. "You truly intend to leave the Pirate Lord's dinner before it even begins?"

"If I must."

"And what would cause such necessity?"

"That largely depends on the Pirate Lord's intentions."

His mouth tilted. "What do you think my intentions are?"

"I think they might well have to do with his newfound knowledge."

"Can you blame me?"

"For your curiosity, no. For the way you've decided to play this particular game..."

"And what game do you think this is? What moves have I made?"

"You invited me here publicly, made me play your little scavenger hunt, and brought me into this room. Of all the places." They cut themself off, pressing their tongue to their teeth. They had no need to admit to Tao that they hadn't been able to move on. They had claimed not to be clingy.

"And what were you expecting? That my finding out who you really are would lead to more of the pleasure we shared? I'm not the one who called that off, Captain." The way he said 'captain' sounded more like an insult than a title.

"You already knew who I really was before you ever found out my family name."

"You say that with such certainty."

"I just don't understand how you can think this revelation changes anything."

"It changes *everything*." He looked over at the painting on the wall with the secret bedroom door. A pair of ships locked in the midst of battle, waves crashing up over the edges of the canvas. The pattern of the wallpaper behind the frame giving the illusion that the waves crashed over the edges of the painting and onto the walls themselves. Nat would offer a lot for the wine hidden behind that painting. "It's true then," Tao murmured. "You are an Adelhard."

"Surely the Adelhard family cannot be that well known," they avoided.

"Is that a yes?"

"I had thought you a little more perceptive than to need to ask such a question."

Tao let out a little, humourless laugh. "You're angry."

"I'm—" Nat huffed out a breath. "This has been a particularly long day for me."

"Your run in with the navy?"

"Just the start." Why was Tao always so easy to talk to?

"The contents of the letter displeased you?"

"I haven't read it."

"Are you going to?"

"Does it matter?"

Tao held up a hand. A gesture of surrender. "Stay for dinner. Tell me what happened with the navy."

Nat examined the tea cup, the way the steam above it rose in swirling circles. Would it be that bad to indulge in even this little closeness? To spend time in this room and pretend, imagine that there was even the possibility that it could lead where it had almost a year ago?

"It was all very dramatic," they started.

Nat was halfway through the story when Tao's people swapped tea for dinner and a larger glass of wine than Nat was used to. They discussed the morality of leaving a ship gutted, full of living crew versus leaving a functional ship with nobody alive.

The first course shifted into the second with yet more wine. The conversation rotated to Nat's predecessor, the captain who had tried and failed to ransom them, skirting the subject itself rather than landing there. It shifted into non-pirates, into people who had made names for themselves in the pirate world.

Nat only noticed the refilling of wine glasses when Tao's turned from empty and discarded on the table to full and in his hand once again. Had he had as much to drink as Nat?

"I'll never forget," Tao began, tilting slightly in a way that didn't seem purposeful.

"Back when I was just a rigger, before I'd even started my apprenticeship as a surgeon, I faced down the most fearsome naval Admiral in all of pirate legend. He had piercing eyes that could see all the way into your soul— I couldn't move for the force of them. He had the deep, booming voice of Davy Jones himself. It hit us like cannons. He and his crew destroyed my ship, killed my captain, and pull the rest of us in for trial. We spent weeks in that brig, no food, no sunlight. The Admiral took great delight in marking us for death." Tao's fingers stumbled over the buttons on his collar before dragging it aside to show a P-shaped scar carved over his collarbone. "I vowed my revenge. Vowed to never forget that name."

Nat shouldn't have drunk the wine. They'd got caught up in talking and flirting and drinking with Tao and now both of them were too intoxicated for a conversation as heavy as this, but neither was sober enough to shift them away.

Tao was too good a storyteller. His voice smooth and pleasing to Nat's ear. With reduced mental capacities, even just a little less than optimum, Nat was enthralled. Drawn forward, Nat found themself asking, "Who was it?"

Tao's dark eyes flashed with lighting as the storm inside him awoke. "Admiral Adelhard."

4

A Cross Between A Quaint Detective And A Poorly Dressed Valet

Nat groaned, rubbing their eyes to try and mitigate the pain that was the way the sun stabbed into them. Their mouth was dry, as if someone had pulled all the moisture out of it and left it hanging like pressure in the air.

They dragged themself over to the wardrobe. It was a good job they hung their clothes in outfit arrangements, because finding the wherewithal to manage putting together something resembling fashion choices might be impossible in the wake of their headache.

A knock interrupted the last few buttons on their tailed waistcoat. What now? All Nat wanted was a drink and maybe some land-made food. They'd trade a whole outfit for a spicy pork bao bun.

Hui rushed in, arms full of maps. Her dark hair had spilled out of its regular bun, hanging over her shoulders and in front of her face. "Help?" she pleaded.

Nat gestured to the desk in the centre of the room.

Hui dropped the maps atop the red leather, revealing her simple blue tunic top. "I ordered new maps to pick up from here and now I don't know which ones are which."

Nat pushed away their thirst and the pain squashing at their head to lean over the maps with Hui. This couldn't take too long, right?

The pattering of rain against the deck drew Nat's attention away from Hui and toward a damp Aleksei entering the cabin without knocking. "Captain, it's not here."

The sun had shifted away from the cabin windows, now streaming through the door behind Aleksei. How long had they been looking at maps? "What's not?"

"The food delivery we paid for."

"You pre-paid?" Nat pointed at a difference in constellations on top of the pair of star charts.

"That's how it works here." Aleksei pushed his hair back, making the damp strands stick up in an ungainly fashion.

Nat looked up at Hui. "Do you mind if I just...?"

Hui nodded, gathering up the newly annotated maps and heading out of the captain's cabin. The door swung shut behind her.

Nat leaned against their desk. "Talk."

"I arranged to have food delivered at dawn. It's midday and we still have no food."

Nat rubbed at their temples. Midday and they hadn't even made it out of the cabin yet. The headache squeezed their skull and the desire to crawl back into bed surfaced. "You sought out the seller?"

"Missing."

"You sent someone to Tao?"

"No."

"No?"

"Why would I?"

"It's his port. He knows everything that happens here. He'll be able to fix the problem." Replenishing supplies in Tao's port had previously been a straightforward event. Tao ran his port like a well-oiled machine, or a well-crewed ship. Which meant if the machine clogged he knew how to fix it... or he had clogged it on purpose.

"You want me to go talk to Tao?" Aleksei hedged.

"It is technically your job."

"I know that. I just..."

Felt uncomfortable around Tao for almost the same reason as Nat. For the same reason it had taken so many months for Nat to be comfortable around Aleksei after they had been voted in as captain.

Aleksei was the loyal kind. He liked having someone to follow, and a captain was a great choice— except his previous captain had been a terrible person. As far as Nat understood it, Aleksei had been leveraged against Tao in the same way he had been leveraged against Nat. The relationship had begun to form, more than begun in Tao's case, the Captain had found out and she had tried to use it to further her own aims.

Neither Nat nor Tao had taken that well.

"I'll go," Nat sighed. "But he's going to know."

"You wouldn't tell him."

"He knows you're the quartermaster. You think he won't deduce that there's a reason for your absence?"

Aleksei looked away.

"But I'm the Captain and I care about you, so I'll go." Even if Nat had their own sordid history with Tao. Even if their head was still pounding from the previous night. Even if Tao had been forever scarred by... But Nat didn't want to think about that. Not right now.

"Thank you," Aleksei whispered.

Nat didn't bother to grab the jacket from where they had placed it by the door. It might well be raining but Shenai was too hot for a jacket like that during the day, rain or not.

They nodded a greeting at the guard who pushed open the massive main door to Tao's palace. Despite the covered veranda, if the wind shifted, the rain would blast straight into that poor guard. The rain itself wasn't heavy, but it was inescapable, soaking through clothing before one even had the chance to register it. Nat's hair dripped down their collar and into their eyes.

Their boot-steps echoed in the surprisingly empty foyer. Where were the bustling citizens, guards, and pirates? Nat couldn't spot a single other person within the room, bright white tiles shining in the light from sconced lamps. The doors to Tao's throne room were, as always, closed.

As Nat approached them, ready to face the Pirate Lord, or at least as ready as they were likely to get today, Noor stepped up to block them. Xyr dark hair sat in loose waves around xyr heart shaped face, swaying softly with her movement. "The Lord is not receiving."

"But it's his receiving hour."

"He is not receiving."

"Is he waiting for someone specific?"

"I couldn't say."

Nat sighed. "It wouldn't happen to be my quartermaster, would it?"

Noor averted xyr gaze. "I couldn't say."

"Then, perhaps you can help me?"

Noor folded xyr arms.

"We arranged for a food delivery that has gone missing and the merchant in question had similarly disappeared."

"Who arranged the order?"

"Quartermaster, why?"

"Coded orders are different."

Nat pressed their tongue against their teeth. "Either way." They worked to keep a measured tone. "It hasn't been delivered."

Noor's shoulders tensed, rising to meet xyr ears. "What time was the delivery arranged for?"

"Dawn."

Noor's shoulders rose even higher, like a turtle trying to retreat into its shell. "If the quartermaster arranged the order, it might be best for the quartermaster to attempt to rectify the situation."

The rain had ceased by the time Nat had finished talking with Noor. Most of the crew on deck of *Mercy's Myth* looked dry and happy as the wet deck glittered like siren scales.

"You're covered in mud."

"I am aware of that, Aleksei!" Nat barged through the cabin door, Aleksei following after, his hands raised in a gesture of surrender. Nat touched the mud crusting their sleeve and trouser leg with a grimace. "I fell."

Slipped in the water running its way away from the Pirate Lord's palace, making the path slippery in a way that Nat, in their frustration, hadn't taken the proper precautions about. They'd toppled sideways into the wet grass and spent the rest of the walk back to the ship with their face burning hot.

Aleksei unlatched Nat's wardrobe, pulling out a clean white shirt and grey trousers.

"Fucking Tao. Fucking Noor. And don't think you're getting out of the blame for this!" Nat stopped unbuttoning their waistcoat to gesture down at their muddy side. "If you had gone up there in the first place, I wouldn't be in this mess."

They took the pile of clothing from Aleksei and stepped behind their privacy screen.

"Did you manage to fix it?" Aleksei asked, turning his back to Nat's privacy screen.

"Nope. He wasn't seeing anyone." They stepped out, cleanly dressed. "And now I look like a cross between a quaint detective and a poorly dressed valet." Why did they even own this outfit?

"The grey trousers were the wrong choice?"

Nat shook their head before realising Aleksei couldn't see them. "No, just..." They sighed. "Just grumbling."

"I'll go fix things with Tao." He tentatively turned around as the bed creaked when Nat perched on it.

They tended to avoid the bed when they weren't alone in the cabin, be it residual leftovers from their upbringing or because people came into the captain's cabin for the captain's help, not because they wanted to see Nat. "I'm sorry."

"You're sorry?"

"Tao is trying to get back at me."

"For?" Aleksei came to sit next to them, the bed sinking slightly under his weight. His thigh brushed against Nat's, sending shooting signals up Nat's spine. It had been so long since anyone had touched Nat like that. Casual contact. Enjoyable contact.

But the lingering doubt pushed at the edges of the desire. The previous captain was gone, but the fact that Aleksei had been willing to use their intimacies like that wasn't something Nat would ever be okay with. Even if the idea of a captain and a quartermaster being in a relationship would have worked.

Aleksei seemed like a relationship sort of person. The kind who would dedicate himself to a partner like he did to the ship. Nat didn't think they could do that. Couldn't trust Aleksei with that part of themself. They couldn't trust anyone with it. Not really.

"Do you remember when I first got here?" they whispered.

"How could I forget?" Aleksei's voice came out husky.

"Your then-captain wanted to know who I was, where I came from, and how she could use that to her own advantage."

Aleksei nodded.

"Tao has learnt some of that. He isn't taking it particularly well. My family... Let's just say he doesn't like them."

5

Not To Make It Sound Too Much Like A Date

With Aleksei off attempting to smooth the whole situation over with Tao —or at least get the food supplies they'd already paid for, Nat finally had the chance to sit at their desk and pull out the letter addressed to a version of themself they thought was lost forever.

On the back sat a wax seal with the Adelhard family crest on it. The same red wax that matched Nat's hair, the same family crest, the same deep black ink and carefully written address on the front. All exactly the same as the letter that had sent Nat to sea. Except this one also had Nat's old name on the front.

Nat peeled it open and let the card within fall free. A card? Not just a letter sealed in wax? How odd. That only happened for...

The delicate paper with perfectly decorated edges seemed to weigh a thousand kilogrammes— heavier than any piece of rigging, heavier than raising anchor alone, heavier than the weight of the secrets Nat had been keeping for such a long time.

Lord and Lady Adelhard

request the honour of your presence

at the wedding uniting their daughter,

Carrolline Adelhard

Nat's hands trembled at the sight of the words at all. They couldn't stand to read any further. Their eyes landed on the tiny scribbled word at the bottom. The most damning piece of it all.

Help

Unmistakably Carrolline's handwriting.

Nat slammed the captain's cabin door open, letting loose a bellow of "Aleksei!"

The crew on deck startled at the noise, staring at their ever-composed captain in a half-buttoned waistcoat. On any other ship it wouldn't have warranted notice, but the crew of *Mercy's Myth* had become accustomed to their Captain's preferences and to see them in such disarray had Kajal peering from the rigging into the cabin behind them to see if it held the reason for their relative state of undress.

When Aleksei didn't materialise, Nat glided across the deck to Bear. The humongous man in neat and tidy clothes seemed to shrink in Nat's wake.

"Where is he?" Nat demanded, the wedding invitation clutched so tightly between their fingers that their hand began to hurt.

"He was in the Lord's Palace," Bear signed.

"Then I will have to pay Tao another visit."

A tap to their shoulder stopped Nat before they reached the boarding plank. Bear gestured to their torso.

"Quite right, Bear. Dressing appropriately is wise."

*N*at had tucked the card into their waistcoat, close to their heart. They tried to shrug off, to push away the feeling of discomfort at their state of dress. What had they been thinking getting this grey ensemble in the first place? They should have changed. Should have picked something else to wear, something that actually made them feel confident, like a shining, glittering, iridescent thing. Like a siren with scales almost as entrancing as their song.

But no. Nat was still attired like the quaint detective poorly dressed valet. That dove grey set that made them feel just a touch too much like someone trying to be masculine. Why had they even bought these?

Throwing open the doors to the throne room, Nat stopped still.

A long table had been brought into the room. Aleksei and Tao sat across from one another, sharing a meal.

"What is going on here?" Nat whispered.

Why was Tao eating in his throne room with Aleksei? Why not his secreted away receiving room? It wasn't like Aleksei hadn't been there before.

Aleksei's head snapped over toward his Captain. Nat knew they were impeccably dressed; Bear had even tied his cravat around their neck for them. A delicate ocean patterned piece that did soften the greyness of the rest of the outfit. But the way Aleksei looked at them screamed of confusion, that there was something about Nat that seemed dishevelled.

"We are preparing to sail," Nat blurted.

Aleksei's eyebrows drew together. He pushed to his feet but stopped there, tethered by the hand resting atop his on the table.

Tao examined Nat, but they turned on their heel and left. They couldn't cope with that focused attention right now. Didn't want to give him to opportunity to ask questions they couldn't hope to answer. Scared to risk the chance that he would see yet more of Nat that he disliked.

Aleksei muttered a quick apology before hurried footsteps chased Nat to the path between the Palace and the Pirate Lord's garden wall.

"What happened?" One short touch to Nat's shoulder blade. They flinched from the memory of pain. "Why the sudden shift? Where are we going?"

Nat paused. Glanced around to ensure they were alone. "I am telling you this as my friend, not as my quartermaster, not as my first mate, not as your captain."

Aleksei's brows were stitched together. He reached out a hand again, as if to provide comfort but stopped before he made contact.

Nat tried not to wince at the attempt. They could only imagine what Aleksei would be putting together in his head, between Nat storming into Tao's palace, not playing their game, speaking so plainly.

"My sister wrote to me."

"Sister?" Aleksei breathed.

"My parents are marrying her off."

"You have parents..."

"Everybody has parents, Lyosha."

"Nat." His hands landed on Nat's shoulders, golden eyes bright as the sun boring into them. "What are you trying to say?"

"We have to go."

"We have to go where?"

"We have to go to the wedding."

"Your sister's wedding?"

"Yes."

"We?"

They paused. "Yes."

Aleksei's eyes narrowed, as if he was peering through a thick fog. "You are inviting me to your sister's wedding?"

"Oh, Sunflower," Nat sighed, slipping into dandy tone like a fish through water. Wrapping the protective persona around themself. "Not to make it sound too much like a date."

"Nat," Aleksei warned.

Nat brushed off Aleksei's warm hands, unable to bear the touch with what they were doing. "I don't know. You, the crew, alone. Whatever way it works out, *I* need to go."

6
At Risk Of Drowning

"Talk to me." Aleksei leaned his back on the railing next to Nat's forearms.

Mercy's Myth had set out, the crew seamlessly settling into their roles aboard. Nat had covered the small jobs that often fell through the cracks before situating themself as they so often did, resting folded forearms on the stern of the ship, watching the wash *Mercy's Myth* left in its wake.

When Nat had left the house after being sent to sea, Carrolline had been a child, she hadn't even been out to society. Nat's last glimpse had been of her desperately crying as she stood at her mother's side while Nat closed the front door behind themself.

"About what?"

"What exactly we're walking into."

Nat dropped their head, letting their curls brush against their hands. Their hair was too long, had been getting too long before the pirates claimed them and had a subsequent year of extra growth on top of that. "I don't know."

"You always know. You don't start fights you don't think you can win."

"You have been by my side almost every day of the last year, have we ever travelled to high society spaces?"

"No."

"Exactly. I don't know what's changed in my absence. I don't know what to expect." They lifted their head and looked out to the sea once again. Their home for almost two full years. "I shouldn't be putting any of you in this position at all."

Or themself.

The idea of taking the crew of *Mercy's Myth* into the hornet's nest of a high society port, let alone one with such strong ties to the navy as Dinium weighed on Nat. Weights like that left you at risk of drowning.

It was dangerous, and they hadn't even asked if the crew would be okay with it. They had just set them all off in the direction of home. Selfish. No better than their predecessor. It rubbed against them like rope burn.

Aleksei let out a long, slow breath. "How are you going to make it up to Tao?"

"Make what up to him?"

"Your behaviour wasn't exactly in line with how one is meant to behave toward the Pirate Lord."

Nat drummed their hands lightly against the ship's rail. "You get on that."

They bounced down the stairs and into the captain's cabin. Sure, they felt bad about how they had behaved toward Tao. But it wasn't like Tao had done nothing worthy of reproach. Why was it Nat's job to appease him?

"Captain!" Aleksei called after them, following them through the closed door.

"Usually if a door is closed, the polite thing to do is knock," Nat chided.

"You expect me to fix this?"

"The crew and my door?"

"You are the captain. You have to parlay with the Pirate Lords."

"Ah, that. Haven't we had this conversation before?"

"Have we?"

When Aleksei and Nat had approached Tao's palace after Nat's captaincy had begun, having been to meet all the other Pirate Lords in an official capacity, Nat had been buzzing with excitement. They had been so ready to see Tao, to present themself and answers to the questions he had hurled at them like insults the last time they had seen each other.

Tao had deigned to get out of his throne, but not with any of the looks Nat expected him to have. He seemed surprised that Nat would return. He had stayed silent long enough for Nat's fizzling excitement to start to singe at the edges. Stayed silent long enough that Nat had lashed out with the statement, "I am not a carousel to be circled over and over."

"Then why are you dressed like one?" he had fired back.

The rejection had burned in their stomach all the way back down the hill to the ship as Aleksei had berated them for angering yet another Pirate Lord. "Tao of all people!" he had hissed.

And that had led to Nat hiding in the captain's cabin for the rest of their stay in Shenai. Trying to avoid it ever since.

Nat rubbed at the spot just above their eyebrow, as if would allow them to pull their thoughts to a stop. "It isn't urgent right now."

"You intend to let it stew? You don't think that will make everything worse?"

"It's not like we can get a letter to him until we hit land anyway."

"So start drafting the letter."

"Who is captain here? You don't make the orders."

Aleksei's left eyebrow rose. "Make the orders?"

"Shut up," Nat grumbled, cheeks heating.

"I thought Endrish was your first language."

"Ne bud' sukoy!"

Aleksei blinked. A smile broke over his face slowly, like the sun appearing from behind the clouds.

"Wouldn't have thought anyone would smile after being told they're being a bitch," Nat teased, crooked smile tilting at their lips.

Aleksei's attention drifted past Nat to the desk. He opened his mouth, undoubtedly to suggest drafting the letter to Tao.

"Lyosha," Nat interrupted. "I can't."

"Why not?"

"Honestly, I'm just trying to make it there right now. He's not the only one feeling awkward. He's not the only one who's been slighted." They tugged the hair off their face. "He knows *everything*. He knows more about my past, my family, than anyone. What am I supposed to say? That I'm sorry? Sorry for what? Being born into the family I was born into? Not telling him sooner? What about the way he's been treating me since then, purely based on that singular piece of knowledge? Does that factor in?"

How could Nat handle knowing that *their father* had branded Tao a pirate? How could they two of them go on from this position? How could their father impact, even destroy, their life so far from anything he was supposed to have touched?

"And then there's where we're going," Nat continued. "My family, Lyosha. I haven't seen them since I left with *The Valiant*. How am I supposed to fit into it now? Do I still fit? How well can I pretend?"

"Do you need to fit back in?"

"Yes. That's how it works back there. If I turn up and see my family, I have to fit back into it." They took a deep breath and rubbed their face. "And what about the crew? I'm trying to take them into a Lander Port, a naval adjacent one at that! And for what? Me. Me and my own selfishness."

"When was the last time you were selfish?"

"What?"

"The last time you didn't immediately come running when the crew made a request of you?"

"That's a captain's job." And after the last captain, Nat had thought it even more vital to emphasise that, to make it plain and clear to every member of the crew that they were a vital piece of the ship and that Nat would be here for them, no matter what.

"Not your predecessor."

"Yes, well, we both know how I feel about her."

7
Not Enough Of A Pirate

Nat had never been enough.

Not enough of an heir for their father with their distractible and dandyish ways. He had wanted someone inclined to naval prowess: strong, fierce, commanding.

Not enough for high society, relegated to the fringes. Nat didn't like to dance, but even if they had they wouldn't have been asked.

Not enough for the navy, always late to inspection and lacking even the most basic knowledge of the inner workings of a ship and its crew.

And certainly not enough for the crew of *Mercy's Myth* who had only chosen Nat for lack of any other option. Nat was still waiting for the day they found someone better and had to figure out how to drop Nat like a hot stone. They hoped it would be kind, somewhere safe and easy to make a new plan from. But Nat's life didn't usually work out that way.

They had never been enough for partners either. Or friends. Interpersonal relationships were a challenge for everyone, but Nat... They liked to claim they hadn't been looking, that they never wanted to marry for love. But it was more a resigned reality than actual want. One too many penny dreadfuls from the second Lady Adelhard had left Nat wondering if there was some perfect person out there who would take their shortcomings in stride. Who would love them not just in spite of these things, but possibly even because of them.

But even if Nat did ever stumble upon such an impossible person as that, they couldn't have offered the same back. Too much time squashing their own wants in favour of everyone else's. Nat wasn't enough because the only other option was to be too much. And not enough was somehow easier. At least people simply forgot about them that way.

Not that the crew would have any chance

of forgetting about them in Dinium if the winds continued their unfavourable battering of the sails. At this rate they wouldn't make it until after the wedding was over and done with. Nat stared out over the stern of the ship, hair twisting in front of their face.

They should tell the crew where they were going, why they were going there. They had been procrastinating, hoping that the whole situation would somehow resolve itself without Nat's intervention at all. But the fact of the matter was that Nat had asked them to go to Dinium and to Dinium they went.

If Nat told them, how would they take it? Would they turn on Nat? Expect Nat to stay forever? Was that what Nat wanted? If they never got there, wouldn't life be so much simpler?

The way the light and the winds played out over the water reminded Nat all too well of their interaction with the sirens, when they had traded a song for safe passage of a ship that wasn't even theirs. Why couldn't all things turn out as simple as that interaction had?

Nat pushed away from the stern of the ship, resolved to tell the crew, or at least the most trusted ones where they were going and why. Partway down the main deck a flash of yellow caught their eye.

"Kajal," they called. "Port side?"

The rigger scrambled over, hanging as far from the rigging as they could get, and pointed over the edge of the ship. "Overboard!"

Nat whipped up a safety line, tied it inexpertly around themself and leapt into the water below.

"Captain!" Aleksei bellowed as Nat crashed into the cold ocean.

Fuck. Why was it always so freezing? They must be closer than Nat had realised. These were not the tropical waters near Shenai.

They tore the tails of their waistcoat away, abandoning it to the currents. No point weighing themself down with extra fabric when the waves were already crashing against them, trying to push them underneath the ship and away from the crew member fallen overboard.

Something tugged at them, pulling them away from the rapidly disappearing pirate. The safety line. Someone was pulling Nat's safety line.

They tried to swim against it but the tug

of the rope came again, too insistent, stronger than their forward motion. A wave smashed over the head of the pirate, dragging them under the surface of the water.

Whoever was on the other end of Nat's safety line had just made this whole situation far worse. Then again, Nat had always been impulsive.

They yanked a knife from their belt and sawed through the line. The rope frayed and, with one more tug from the ship, Nat was swimming freely. They gasped in a breath and dipped below the surface of the water. The darkness of the ocean hid most things from Nat's salt-stung eyes. They bobbed up to gasp down more air before trying again.

A flutter of yellow caught their eye, and shining silver.

Shit. Sirens?

No matter. Nat pushed against the ocean swell toward the yellow. The need to breathe tugged on their lungs but, unwilling to lose sight of their crewman, Nat barely dared to blink as they sank deeper into the frigid water.

Reaching out a desperate hand, Nat's fingers clasped around a sodden shirt. They furiously kicked their legs, drawing both humans up toward the surface.

Swirling silver spun and circled them. Not sirens, sea monsters. Adult ones could swim in these spirals fast enough to turn anything between them into a whirlpool worthy of Scylla and Charybdis. But these ones were small, adolescent or even juvenile. Still, they tugged.

Nat's lungs screamed for air. Their fingers dug further into the fabric between them even as the selfish, life-preserving part of their brain, the piece that sounded too much like the kind of people who always ended up hurting Nat, begged them to let him go. Let go of the pirate, give him to the sea serpents and save themself.

Their head breached the surface. Their limbs shook as they panted for air. But it wasn't over yet. Safety line gone, Nat still needed to make it back to the ship. The limp form in their arms dragged at them, didn't seem to be breathing. The sun beat down on both of them, too bright on still stinging eyes.

A stream of red arced down toward Nat in the water. The ocean swell drew it out to them. Fabric. A rope. A lifeline. Nat tied it around their crew member's torso and tugged twice.

Treading water as the crew pulled up their fallen mate, Nat battled against the current or the serpents trying to drag them away. Waves washed against the sides of *Mercy's Myth* and swept back over Nat's head, pulling them in too many directions. The cold water stiffened Nat's already overworked muscles as they tried to place each breath with utmost care.

Death was a reality at sea. Every fight brought the potential of it and, while deeply terrifying, at least it would be quick. Unless you were Bear, in which case one fight gone wrong had turned into months of physical healing and more than a few emotional scars to go with his single, prominent physical one. Death by drowning, though...

A wave crashed over Nat's head as they took a breath, forcing salt water down their throat. Nat coughed. But trying to remain upright, and coughing, and fighting the current's pull proved more than Nat could take. A wave carried Nat under the water.

There was a peace to it. Some level of intrinsic and inherent calm that came with the knowledge that the fight was over. This was it. No more of what Tao had called 'the battle that is life'. No more scrabbling to somehow keep going.

But by luck, or fate, or the rejection of juvenile sea serpents, or even one too many trips to the seaside as a child where Nat had exploited the lack of expectation put upon them and learnt to swim and float and bask in the water's soft or violent sloshing, their head popped up from under the waves once more.

The arc of red came again, landing in a white swell. The waves tugged it toward Nat and they reached numb hands out to grab it.

They slammed into the deck, coughing against the salt water scratch all the way into their lungs. Their body trembled against the chill of ocean-soaked clothes and skin. Stumbling to their feet, they dragged themself over to check on the rescued crew member.

Instead, they were treated to Aleksei's hands at their waistcoat lapels, his face pressed close to theirs, jaw clenched tight. "What the fuck were you thinking?"

"Where's—?"

"With Nafia. And that is not the point." He glanced around at the clustered crew then swapped his hand from Nat's lapels to their wrist and tugged them into the captain's cabin.

"What were you thinking?" he demanded as soon as the door clicked shut behind them.

Nat glanced down at the puddle they were dripping onto the floor. Every beam on the ship was treated against water damage, but Nat had never considered that the captain's cabin would have that protection. Should they retreat the wood?

There was some Coded Pirate magic —or maybe just science Nat didn't understand yet— that prevented the rest of the boards on the ship from allowing any water in. Naval ships had bilge pumps; the most hated job on the ship was being set to the bilge, clearing the water out of the lowest levels of the ship. But *Mercy's Myth* didn't need that; it had some special thing that the Pirate Queen kept secret until a ship got Coded. But whether that particular special quality had been applied to the captain's cabin was a question Nat hadn't considered before.

"You cut your safety line!" Aleksei tugged at the frayed and snapped rope still wrapped around Nat.

They should take that off. Their fingers were slow to respond.

"What were you thinking!"

"I was thinking to rescue the crew." Nat's voice scraped up their throat like claws.

"One crew member is not worth the captain's life. We could have lost both of you with a stunt like this!"

"Well if *someone* —you, I'm guessing— hadn't pulled the line before I was ready this wouldn't have been a problem."

Aleksei yanked the safety line from around Nat's chest and tossed it aside. His voice dropped. "The current in this area is too strong and it's known to attract sea serpents. Any pirate knows that!"

"Then I guess I'm not a very good pirate, am I?" Nat fired back. Their body was back at trembling. "But we already knew that."

"What exactly is that supposed to mean?"

Nat shook off the weights that wanted to drag them deeper into the ocean than they had just been. Bad pirate. Bad captain. Bad heir. "It means you don't even trust me. How much is it going to take? What is it I need to do for you to stop behaving like I'm going to turn into *her* or like I'm still some walking cash? Like I'm just playing a game here?"

"I do trust you."

"I've yet to see any evidence of that. You all look at me and see that person, that high society, naval grunt, *dandy*," —they used the word the way it had so often been fired at them, as if it was an insult rather than an identity— "Who stood on that very deck as your Captain—" The words dissolved into a fit of coughing bringing up salty water that Nat didn't think could still be there.

Aleksei rubbed a hand across their back. "We should get Nafia to check on you."

Answer enough.

8

Do You Have An Invitation?

Nat tapped the wedding invitation, slightly battered from the sea water thanks to their unintended swim with sea-serpents, but once again tucked into the inside pocket of their waistcoat: a delicate black and silver patterned number with matching trousers and elegant knee-length jacket typically worn by nonbinary members of society. They adjusted the cuffs of their scarlet shirt, they had chosen the colour in the hope it would provide them confidence, but it proved nothing to the imposing stone face of Adelhard Manor.

Nerves bubbled up in Nat's throat like the last breath of a drowning sailor.

In the evening light, the dark grey stones of the manor loomed over them, gold eyes of lit windows staring out into the gardens and onto the driveway. A monster from mythical tales with eyes enough to see all your faults and flaws. The door sat inside a well-lit alcove, the lantern swinging in the slight breeze, a dizzying sway all too much like that swinging lantern in the cells below deck when Nat had been imprisoned on the ship they now commanded. The gaping maw of the monster.

The brass door knocker seemed lighter than the last time they had lifted it. Was it the physical strength gained from their time working on ships? Or could Nat just not feel their arms because they were holding their breath?

Sucking in a gulp of air through their nose, Nat's chest puffed up just as the butler opened the door. His grey hair lay in lines over his head, his black suit impeccably, impossibly clean, not even a stray piece of fluff or hair. His shoes ever so slightly overshined not stepping through the door frame and onto the Adelhard family crest mosaic that filled the alcove floor.

His wrinkled face frowned at Nat, summoning memories of being a teenager and walking the line of rebellion. "Do you have an invitation?"

"I should think the returning Liege wouldn't need an invitation to enter their own home." Nat's ever-useful dandified tone came out strangely haughty. It rang wrong in Nat's ears. This was all wrong. They wanted to cringe. But they stood straight and waited.

Brett blinked, eyes darting up and down Nat's form. Was he struggling to recognise them? Had they changed that much in such a short time?

Finally, he stepped aside to allow Nat and their few companions enter. Nat removed the hat from their head, handing it to the old man they tried not to look too closely at the tiled entryway, at the mirror over the chest of drawers by the door that Nat had never learnt the purpose of.

The curtains had changed. No longer decorated with yellow flowers. These ones had golden bells. It shouldn't have mattered.

It did.

Brett disappeared with the three hats and a single coat, not bothering to direct Nat and their guests to the location of the event evidently behind hosted by the Adelhard family that night. Even if Nat hadn't known the way, they would have been able to follow the noise of it.

Standing in the doorway of the Adelhard ballroom, Nat took in the familiar and unfamiliar elements. The pale wood floors, the huge windows lining one wall, the delicate gas lamp chandeliers. The curtains had changed in here too. And the layout wasn't one Nat was familiar with. But it was undoubtedly the space in which Nat had grown up. The huge room in which they had tugged off their shoes to slide around with only socks on their feet. The one in which they'd dashed from one end to the other in a desperate attempt to escape some tutor or other. The room in which they had been introduced to society.

The attendees, both new and well known, milled around the room, talking and dancing and nibbling at the array of provided food tabled along the northern wall.

A laugh drew their attention to a group near the door. The dandy's hand was splayed over his heart and his double-layered purple and cream waistcoat. That style was new. But Lord Roydon had always been either the cutting edge of fashion or stratospherically out of fashion.

His other hand landed on the bare shoulder of a woman dressed in an elegant, if hugely skirted, pink gown more befitting an unmarried young woman than the mother of a woman of marriageable age. Her hair had been piled atop her head in a way that reminded Nat of nothing so much as an ill-folded blanket on a shelf. Her head tossed back in the laugh she shared with Lord Roydon exposed the long column of her throat, coated in a frankly gaudy amount of jewels.

Nat's heart froze in their chest.

She lowered her chin once again, glancing toward the doorway. For one precious second, her smile faltered.

She politely excused herself from conversation with Lord Roydon, whose attention stayed pinned to her even as the rest of the group continued their conversation.

"No cravat?" she greeted.

The red cravat that had matched this shirt was the one Aleksei or Kajal had thrown into the water as a signal of where the rope line was. Which Nat hadn't realised until far too late into their outfit choice. They had already been running dangerously close to uncouthly late, particularly trying to convince one of their self-defined bodyguards into decent attire.

"Do you really think it wise to begin an engagement regarding clothing choices?" Nat shot a pointed look at the dress.

It was all too easy to slip back into the haughty arrogance that had once been the core of Nat's persona. What they wouldn't give to have done this out of sight of the crew of *Mercy's Myth*.

Lady Adelhard's hostess smile didn't falter but her eyes had narrowed to slits. "I had thought you would not make it back from your gallivanting to see your sister's engagement."

Better or worse than 'we all thought you were dead'?

"Do you truly believe I wouldn't do everything in my power to return for it?"

"It has been an awfully long time."

"Unfortunate circumstances beyond my control."

"Unfortunate circumstances..." Lady Adelhard echoed. The accent shift rang in Nat's ears. Had they used to speak in such a painfully rounded way? When at that stopped? Where had Nat picked up the easy contractions? When?

Lady Adelhard shook her head briefly and gestured at the pair flanking Nat.

"Ah, yes. Allow me to introduce Mr Aleksei Fyodorovich Zima." Nat's hand glided in the air in front of Aleksei, from his chin to his waist.

Nat had seen Aleksei dressed nicely exactly once. When he had come to bargain for their return to the mercy of the captain who had captured them. That held nothing to now. Usually he was in what Nat termed a state of undress: low slung trousers, boots if he was off the ship, and a poorly buttoned shirt if it was cool enough to require one. Now, however, his shirt collar clung to his neck with an elegantly understated cravat including pin that was more of a weapon than a fashion choice. His waistcoat hugged his torso, bordering on too small —which made sense since it was one of Nat's. His jacket displayed his shoulders, sculpted by years of ship work. Simple, plain fabrics put together so elegantly and well —if Nat did say so themself— that the plainness had become a feature.

In the carriage ride from the docks to Adelhard Manor, he had been tugging at the shirt collar and cravat like a toddler. Nat snuck a quick glance to ensure he wasn't doing that now. A small crease had taken up residence between his pale eyebrows, making him look far older than usual. But at least his hands sat quietly at his sides.

Lady Adelhard greeted Aleksei carefully, proffering a gloved hand for him to kiss.

He shook it.

"And," Nat cut in before anything worse could happen, or they could start laughing. "Lord— uh — B—"

Bear's hands flashed into finger spelling.

"B—asil— Lord Basilton," Nat translated quickly.

Bear was always a looming presence by the sheer size of him. Twice as wide as Aleksei and at least a head taller. He wore his cravat high and tight on his neck, giving the impression of modestly. Nobody else need know he was hiding the glaring scar that slashed across the column of his throat. He usually didn't care who saw, but Nat couldn't say they didn't understand the need for privacy in high society.

Bear's attire was all his own. Pieces he'd collected in the time that Nat had been captaining the ship. They didn't exactly match, but they melded seamlessly into a particular impression of a person. He'd even pulled his long hair into a ponytail at the nape of his neck. Hopefully nobody would notice that it was tied with a thin piece of rope rather than ribbon.

Nat wanted to ask so many questions about the name. The only reason anyone on the ship called him Bear was that Nat had entitled him 'the bear man' when they first met. Was Basilton his old name? The one he hadn't previously been willing to share? Was it just a name he came up with? Someone he knew? Was it what he wanted to be called? Or just a code for however long he remained in high society?

He greeted Lady Adelhard with an elegant hand kiss as part of a bow.

"A pleasure to make your acquaintance," he signed. Nat verbalised for him.

"What is he doing with his hands?" Lady Adelhard hissed.

"Bear can't speak, he uses sign language to communicate," Nat clarified.

"Oh... How novel."

"Novel? What happened to Miss Hayes?" She had been the one to teach Nat the base sign they had known when first meeting Bear.

"She married and moved to Breeten. They say the sea air is good for her health. Do tell your friend it is a pleasure to meet him."

"He can hear perfectly well." Nat's irritation blasted through the dandy tone. Too real. And a poor show all around. They affixed their dandy-neutral expression to their face. It came as a struggle. "Gentlemen, may I present Lady Adelhard." They took a breath. This was it. No turning back. Telling Aleksei and Bear. "My father's wife and the hostess of this event."

"Not your mother?" Bear asked.

Nat shook their head.

"I am sure your sister will be happy to know you have arrived home," Lady Adelhard interjected. "She is around... somewhere."

"Is there anyone else I should keep an eye out for?"

Lady Adelhard's face tightened almost imperceptibly. "Your father dipped away for some business. I'm sure he will be back soon."

He'd gone off to bed then. A wash of relief swept through Nat. That was a meeting they would rather postpone as long as possible. "No fiancé?"

"Sadly he could not attend tonight."

Nat tried not to frown. What kind of fiancé didn't turn up to an event like this? Most engaged folks wanted as much time together as possible before the wedding went ahead. The image of the rapidly scrawled 'help' at the base of Nat's invitation flashed in their mind. Something was going on here and Nat intended to get to the bottom of it before any weddings could take place.

Lady Adelhard stepped away, returning to her previous group. Lord Roydon was no longer a part of it. Nat searched the ballroom for his familiar face.

Lady Bakshi drew their attention instead, just as she always had. Another dandy, zeroing in on Nat just as quickly as they had on her. Judging by the wicked smile that stole over her face, she wasn't too angry at Nat's sudden disappearance or equally surprising reappearance. Then again, she had inside information about Nat's disappearance that, hopefully, hadn't been made public.

9

How Did Our Hummingbird Find Exeunt From A Pirate Ship?

With all the time Nat had spent in and around busy docks, ports, and ships, their ability to shift through a crowd hadn't rusted with time away from balls. They picked up pieces of conversation as they went, slipping into that habit just as easily as every other.

"— can't believe they're throwing the ball without the fiancé—"

"—Shameful to wear a dress like that at her age—"

"New people, I haven't seen them before—"

"—Apparently, he's lost at sea."

"Isn't that the lost Adelhard?"

"You," Lady Bakshi accused when Nat came to a stop by her, "have been gone the longest time!"

"Your outfit is incredible."

The mustard yellows, golds, and pinks that made up Lady Bakshi's wonderful amalgamation of a sari and a ball gown enhanced her deep brown skin and made her long black hair gleam. "Thank you." She curtsied. "You've changed."

Nat looked down at their scarlet shirt and black and silver suit. "I'll admit to being a tad under-prepared for a ball."

"I never thought I'd see the day," Lady Bakshi laughed lightly. "Liege Nat Adelhard admitting something, and only wearing one primary colour."

Nat couldn't help but smile at that. "There were plenty of days I only wore one primary colour— albeit, usually combined with a multitude of secondary colours, but with age comes wisdom and, potentially, the desire to be a little less flashy."

"We have been sorely missing your sense of humour these last few years. Nobody plays the game like you."

"I claim insult," Liege Mishra muttered. Nat almost hadn't noticed xem with the way xyr outfit matched the upholstery in the room.

"Oh hush." Lady Bakshi waved a hand at xem. "There were rumours," she said to Nat. "That you had been captured by pirates."

Nat forced that dandy smile back into place. It stretched their mouth in strange ways. How was this so different to verbally sparring with Tao? Why did this feel so awkward? Were they just out of practice? "Do you truly believe if I had been captured by pirates I could have returned for my sister's engagement and wedding?"

"Of course not. I am not so foolhardy as to think you would have any exeunt from a pirate ship!"

"Do tell dear..." Lord Roydon inserted himself into the group, laying a delicate hand on Nat's forearm as he searched for an appropriate nickname. His mouth was frozen on the beginning of the word 'lambkin'. It didn't fit. "What is going on with those two burly gentlemen attempting to make their way over to you?"

"Those are my... associates."

"Might you consider introducing them to the room?"

He hadn't removed his hand from their arm. Nat's fingers twitched to shift it. But that wasn't the done thing.

Pirates made contact for all sorts of reasons. Friends embraced freely: leaning on one another, tickling and nudging and touching. Crew brushed up against each other: support, safety, necessity.

Acquaintances and foes made contact to hurt or contain.

Nat, having been prisoner and now captain, rarely felt more than a hand on their shoulder, and even those didn't typically stay long. Nat had been itching for contact ever since that night that had landed them on the edge of a scandal the last time they had stood in a ballroom like this. Tiny brief interludes hadn't been enough, could never be. And yet... Lord Roydon's hand on their arm felt like a foe. Like the previous captain. Like Grigg. Like the hand of a naval officer.

Dangerous.

Unwanted.

But they were friends. At least they had been.

"Lyosha, Bear, may I introduce Lord Kingston Victor Roydon, Lady Rajni Bakshi, and Liege Jothi Mishra."

"It's Lady Mishra now," Lady Bakshi corrected.

Nat fumbled for words as Aleksei's attention fixed on each dandy in turn.

"You're married?"

Lady Bakshi— Lady Mishra laughed. "To Jothi's older brother. It's been, what? Six months now."

Nat swallowed thickly. Married. Rajni was married.

Lord Roydon cleared his throat and tilted his chin at Aleksei and Bear.

"Forgive me. Old friends, this is Mr Aleksei Fyodorovich Zima, and Lord Basilton."

"How did our little hummingbird meet a Kovian?" Finally Lord Roydon shifted his hand from Nat's arm. Only to place it atop Aleksei's.

Aleksei looked at the hand on his arm, at Nat, and then to Lord Roydon. "How did you know?"

His accent seemed more prominent than on the ship, but Nat couldn't tell if it was just the context of being surrounded by perfectly practised, high society Endrish accents instead of the mishmash of accents on the ship.

"My mother's family is Kovian. She taught me the naming patterns." He looped his arm through Aleksei's and swapped languages.

Nat wanted to reach out, to warn Aleksei that talking with a dandy held inherent risks that Aleksei had never been particularly skilled at guarding himself against. But they had no way to do so. Not here. Not now.

They brushed down their waistcoat, invitation in their pocket crinkling under their touch.

Aleksei would just have to take care of himself. Nat hadn't asked him to come tonight. Hadn't asked either of them. Bear had turned up on the deck of *Mercy's Myth* in full formal attire and Aleksei had appeared in, to his credit, a fully buttoned shirt. Each had demanded to come, claimed it was dangerous to go alone. As if it wasn't equally dangerous to bring pirates into the lair of dandies.

Across the room, an elegant, understated daisy-heart yellow gown embroidered with blue flowers —forget-me-nots— caught and held Nat's attention. Shoving thoughts of Aleksei, Bear, the ship, Lady Bakshi-Mishra, and Tao out of their head, Nat wove their way across the ballroom. More compelled by this dress than they had been even by sirens.

10
Simply Collateral Damage

"You're here!" A squeal, a beam, and Nat was glad of their ship-trained strength when Carrolline leapt into their arms just as she had as a proper child. Not this young lady.

"Of course I'm here, you're getting married!" They put Carrolline back on her own two feet.

Nat would have been able to describe their baby sister in such great detail a portrait artist would have been able to depict her perfectly. Every difference, every tiny change stood out starkly to them. Her face was slimmer, her hair darker more of a chocolate or tree-bark brown than the appropriately soil-coloured tresses she'd had before. It had then matched the grass stains on her knees. Now it gave an air of luxury about her, made her skin look paler, more like it matched the fairness of Nat's own.

Carrolline led Nat out into the promenading garden, rectangular in shape and as large as the ballroom itself. Its strategic, elegant lawns and variety of trees cast interesting shadows from the light shining through the long windows from the inside of Adelhard Manor. The pleasantly chilled air brushed at Nat's hair, freeing it from where they had tried to contain it purely by the roughness of salt-sturdied strands.

She took a seat on the bench beneath the twisted tree that sat in the very centre of the garden. Just outside the reaches of the light.

Nat pulled the invitation from their waistcoat pocket and sank down on the bench next to her.

Carrolline looked at it and turned her face away, a practiced move to avoid looking at evidence and preserve a demure appearance. Nat knew the move. It was one of Rajni's.

They let the silence grow and prickle at the back of their neck.

"I was just nervous," Carrolline blurted. "I'm sure everything will be fine. I am sure I just wanted attention."

"Carrolline, if this marriage is not something you want, there are options."

"Options," she laughed. "What options do not ruin my reputation? What options when *you* disappeared and left me the only person to find someone to inherit everything?"

"I didn't leave of my own accord.

"Does it matter? You never came back!"

"I'm back now."

Carrolline huffed.

"Oh, come on, Cottontail."

Despite her pretence, a broad grin spread over Carrolline's face at the old nickname.

"You could at least catch me up on what I've missed."

Carrolline leaned her weight against Nat's shoulder and began regaling them with the petty grievances, arguments, marriages, and scandals that had occurred while Nat had been away at sea.

Nat could have stayed there forever. Letting Carrolline's voice wash over them with the comfort of home. But yellow light spilled out of a newly opened door, spoiling the dark seclusion of the night.

"Carrolline?" Lady Adelhard called from the doorway.

Carrolline winced and jumped to her feet. She brushed her hands down the bodice of her gown in a move Nat was acutely and uncomfortably familiar with, affixed a pleasant smile to her face, and approached her mother.

"Please tell me you have not been out here alone, Carrolline! It is shameful enough that you are found missing from your own engagement party, but to be out here alone would be entirely too much."

"Once again, my presence surprises you." Nat stepped out of the shadows and into the circular glow escaping the inside of the house, into Lady Adelhard's sight line.

"Go inside, Carrolline," Lady Adelhard ordered, stepping aside to allow her daughter to slip through the door.

She didn't look back. Carrolline never did.

"You." Lady Adelhard stepped toward Nat, the door swinging closed behind her, secluding the pair in the same darkness that had been close with Carrolline. That privacy now screamed of threat. She hissed her words with a venom Nat was all too familiar with. "You may have spoilt your own prospects with your actions and your absence and your sudden reappearance with two male escorts to a ball, for which you had no invitation, I might add. But I will die before I allow you to ruin my daughter's reputation!"

To their surprise, the venom still wheedled it way into them, pushing their shoulders to sink. Nat fought to keep their voice neutral. "I have no intention of harming my sister."

"Then might I advise you keep to yourself. Obviously you will stay here; this is technically your home. Nevertheless, I implore that you keep your distance from my daughter. It was difficult enough to sweep your indiscretions under the rug, to explain away your sudden desire to take up a naval life—"

"My desire?" Nat scoffed.

"If Carrolline is seen fraternising with you, it could bring all those things back under the spotlight and this marriage may well fall apart before it begins." She turned to walk back into the house.

Maybe, once, that would have been the end of the conversation. But Nat was no longer quite the same person they were when they left. "Did you bother to ask her if she wants this?"

Lady Adelhard froze, hand on the door.

"Dare I ask if you have even met this man yourself? Or whether it's a scheme your husband began? And for what purpose? The gentleman in question must have some particular desirable trait. Of course, without meeting him it is hard for you to say." The light sigh that escaped with that final statement made Nat's stomach clench. This was cruel. Why were they doing this?

Lady Adelhard whipped around to glare at Nat, eyes blazing under the moonlight. "Don't you dare," she warned.

"Dare what?" Nat snapped. Lady Adelhard's venom might still have bite, but Nat wasn't who they had been the last time that venom had bitten. "Point out the problems? Shine a light on your own issues? Try to protect my sister from a marriage that could well be worse than unintentional spinsterhood? —Not that Carrolline is anywhere near the age one might consider her a spinster. You speak of my indiscretions as if her marrying at this age isn't a red flag on its own. You want my help, tell me the plan."

"It is none of your business."

"That's fine," Nat huffed, almost a laugh but there was no humour in it. "I know the plan. Marry Carrolline off to some nice naval officer— he is a naval officer is he not?"

"He is."

"Once that marriage is complete, Carrolline will have forged the connection the Her Majesty's Navy that I never could create. The Adelhards are back in the Navy and all the achievements of this man are laid squarely at your husband's feet. Not only that, but Carrolline ceases to be a problem should she share any of my proclivities. All benefit, no downfalls."

"No downfalls?" Lady Adelhard's voice was tight.

"Apologies, I meant no downfalls for *him.* After all, to a man like your husband, everyone else is simply collateral damage."

11
Seems To Be A Lot Of That Going Around

Nat smoothed their hands down the burgundy waistcoat they'd found in the wardrobe. Burgundy! What had possessed them to purchase a burgundy waistcoat? Only a very particular sort looked good in burgundy and the type that flushed as red as their hair when warm was not it.

The waistcoat didn't even fit. It was the only one that would still go over Nat's shoulders. But it didn't fit anywhere near so nicely as it had before. Back when Nat had last lived here, it had hugged their frame, hinting at shapes hidden beneath. Now it stretched and gaped and gave Nat the feeling that somebody with heavy boots stood on their chest.

But that may have been more to do with the situation than the waistcoat.

They tugged again at where the waistcoat caught against the decorative buttons of their trousers. Morning waistcoat with evening-event trousers were hardly a fitting match purely by shape. It wasn't that Nat had any particular favour for the black and silver trousers, while they were an elaborate and beautiful pair that Nat had been saving for a special occasion —perhaps one of the Frozen Wastes Pirate Lord's banquets— it was just that Nat couldn't find any other trousers that fit.

How had they changed so much in such a short time? It wasn't like Nat was still growing. They'd come out to society a little late, not enough to raise questions, easily explained away by their mother's untimely death, but definitely straddling that border. Of course, the reason actually lay, as so many things did, with their father. Still, coming out at twenty, as a Liege was perfectly normal. It actually sat in that perfect periphery where coming out was still appropriate for any gender. Young men tended to come out between nineteen and twenty-five, expected to find a wife and settle down far faster than their binary counterparts. Young ladies between sixteen and twenty-two, given a little more time to settle into society, expected to take a few years before they began to think on settling down. Any woman married before twenty years of age was... bordering on scandal.

Nat set their shoulders. Carrolline wasn't twenty yet. If the Adelhards wanted to claim they needed Nat gone to avoid scandal, they were doing an awfully pale job of keeping themselves on the up-and-up.

The dining room doors stuck when Nat pushed against the heavily decorated wood. Nat's old, plain, white shirt pulled over their shoulders, waistcoat digging into their collarbone as they forced the door over the rug. A different one. They tried not to think about it.

Breakfast lay on the table served on plates with a pattern Nat didn't recognise; toast in a rack, boiled eggs in a plate designed purely for such purpose, kippers and cold meats, and a humongous pot of tea that definitely didn't match the rest of the crockery.

Four places had been set. The head, its immediate left and right, and one more place on the right hand side of the table.

Lady Adelhard had already taken her place at the immediate right of the head of the table, once again wearing a dress more befitting a younger woman. She didn't look up as Nat stumbled to a halt on the other side of the doors.

Propriety said Nat needed to sit opposite her. Propriety sucked.

The way the early morning light combined with the wall lamps shone over the table reminded Nat more of Tao's throne room than it did of their childhood home. They took a deep breath.

"You did not bring your own clothing?" Lady Adelhard asked, not lifting her face from the morning's paper.

"Peaches," Nat injected a sense of humour into their tone. "These are my clothes, in the same way that this is my house."

She pursed her lips. "You have changed, at least in form, perhaps you own new clothes."

"It would hardly have been appropriate to turn up to an event with trunks of clothing, now would it?"

"So they are...?"

"I am sending for them this morning."

Because Lady Adelhard had demanded Nat stay here whether they had wanted to or not. The ball had wound down, people had begun heading home, and Lady Adelhard had gripped so tightly to Nat's arm as she waved people away that Nat had been surprised to find it unbruised this morning.

Carrolline slipped through the door before another word could be spoken. Her morning dress caught to the latch, the delicate lace ready to tear.

"Will father be joining us?" she asked as she freed herself. Had she chosen the embroidered violets as a message? Or just because she liked them? She had worn forget-me-nots the previous night, maybe florals were in fashion. But...

"Of course." Lady Adelhard put the paper to one side.

Nat's heart beat against their rib cage the same way Felitabby had beat against the cell bars below deck of the ship that was now called *Mercy's Myth.* That was, of course, before the then-captain had run him through with a sword.

Nat should have sought out Lord Adelhard the previous night. With the relative safety of a public event at their back. They should have leaned casually against the door of whatever room he was in and told him they were back.

But they hadn't. And, of course he would come to breakfast in his own house. It would be absurd to assume otherwise.

The dining room door burst open with a loud squeak, as if in protest to the latest addition. Once fit, Lord Adelhard had settled well into his retirement with the gut to prove it. He strode past Nat to the head of the table without so much as a glance. The tidy beard decorating his chin had started to grey, dampening the fiery ginger it had been before. Nat's fingers shifted up to touch their own bright red hair before they could think the action through. Unlike Lord Adelhard's limp, straight strands, Nat's hair held a solid corkscrew formation.

Taking his seat at the head of the table, Lord Adelhard reached immediately for both toast and the paper discarded by his wife mere seconds before his arrival. And with his beginning to eat came the flurry of activity as everybody else reached for their favoured breakfasts.

"How was the ball?" he asked, focus glued to the paper.

"Quite the event," Lady Adelhard answered, serving him and Carrolline tea before setting the pot down with its handle facing away from Nat. "Though there were a few unexpected guests."

Nat wasn't too busy helping themself to the little fruit on the table to notice Lady Adelhard's dramatic eyebrows. They shot a glance at Carrolline who bit her lip, shoulders rising in a desperate attempt not to laugh.

"I have faith you handled it perfectly." All Nat could see of Lord Adelhard from this angle were the fingers of the hand wrapped around the paper. Wrinkled and a little hairy with the family signet ring on his little finger. His hand seemed more weathered than when Nat had left. Not that they had tended to pay much attention to his hands. "Terribly rude of them, turning up without proper notice."

"And without invitation." Lady Adelhard's eyebrows had calmed in favour of gesturing with her pointed pile of hair.

"Indeed?" Lord Adelhard sipped his tea. "What is society coming to? A little more milk please, dear."

"Of course, I couldn't turn anyone away."

"No no, that would be improper," Lord Adelhard muttered, clearly paying his wife no mind.

Nat smoothed jam over their slightly chilled toast. Nobody served toast in the world of pirates. The closest Nat had had in years were the warm, filled bread buns from Shenai.

Lady Adelhard made three more attempts as Nat helped themself to two eggs, a slice of bacon, and some kippers, all largely ignored by her husband before she finally gave up and turned to Carrolline.

"Mother," Carrolline said, finally granted attention enough to begin conversation. "Did you see Lord Quibble visited the ball last night?"

"Did he indeed? I can't say I noticed."

"Yes. He spent the majority of the time with Liege Mishra. I believe him sweet on xem."

"How foolish, child," Lady Adelhard scolded. "Lord Quibble could not possibly marry Liege Mishra. He is the eldest of his family line, it would be entirely inappropriate to match with that... dandy." The word *dandy* held the weight of an insult. Used as if it were interchangeable with nonbinary. As if it was Liege Mishra's dandy identity and not xyr gender that made the match inappropriate. Not that Lady Adelhard —or anyone with even a hint of common decency would be so uncouth as to say as much out and out. But the potential that Quibble and Mishra would be unable to produce their own little heirs, either leaving it for Quibble's nephews to inherit —if he had any— or leaving the estate and family line to languish and die out was something that plagued every mother's thoughts in this day and age.

Lieges could inherit, if necessary. But if any of the Lady Adelhards had managed to produce a son for her husband, Nat would have lost top billing as their father's heir regardless of age. But with there only being themself and Carrolline...

In polite society, Lieges and Mxs married second born at the highest, that way inheritance disputes could be avoided altogether. It was just easier that way. And it had become the expected thing.

"I admit I was disappointed that Lydia couldn't make it," Carrolline continued.

"Carrolline, you are to be married soon, you must begin referring to people by their titles and not in the childish way of first names."

"Miss Harcroft then." Carrolline pouted. "She always has the most interesting outfits."

"It's probably best that she missed it. You would rather not be upstaged at your own event."

"She is my best friend, mother. She would never intentionally upstage me."

"She has rather too strong a preference for violets, I think."

"According to this," Lord Adelhard burst out, covering the sound of Nat choking on their tea. "There have been pirates sighted near our very own port."

"Pirates?" Lady Adelhard squeaked.

Nat's fingers itched to snatch the paper from Lord Adelhard, to gather as much information as possible. Their feet begged to run down to the port and check on *Mercy's Myth*. They should never have brought the crew here!

"A ship bearing the moniker of *The Sea Shanty* was spotted last night, rapidly approaching and retreating from shore," Lord Adelhard continued.

Nat found their breath. Not their ship. Not their crew. *The Sea Shanty*? Who captained that? Was it even Coded? A name like that sounded more merchant than pirate.

"Perhaps it will be enough to draw our favourite Captain home," Lady Adelhard responded. "That he might be formally be presented to Carrolline."

"We can only hope, my dear. But he was meant to have been back by now."

"You mean to say he is lost at sea!"

"Seems to be a lot of that going around," Nat muttered.

The paper fell from Lord Adelhard's fingers, landing indelicately in his teacup.

Nat spread strawberry jam over a now-cold slice of toast. They didn't want it, just needed something to do, something to give the air of calm nonchalance. As if their presence should be no surprise. As if it was normal.

Of course, their face betrayed them with the way it burned like they had done something worthy of embarrassment rather than just speaking nine simple words to their father.

"This is not something to joke on," Lady Adelhard hissed.

"The paper is becoming damp." Nat pointed at the tea stain spreading up the page.

Nobody moved.

"What are you doing here?" Lord Adelhard breathed.

"Last I checked this was my family home."

Lord Adelhard surged to his feet and poked a weathered finger toward Nat's face. "You, come with me."

Abandoning the remains of breakfast, paper still discarded in his teacup, Lord Adelhard stomped from the room.

Nat wiped their mouth delicately with a napkin, excused themself, and, with fingers gripping their shirt cuffs almost tight enough to rip, followed Lord Adelhard.

12

Ruining, Ruinous, Ruiner, Ruined

When Nat had left this house, they hadn't expected to be gone long. Six months. A year at a push. Enough time to let the scandal settle. Enough to let tempers cool. They would have fit back into the gap that had barely begun to close at the edges. They would have held to the pretence that they wanted to explore naval life, that it was a character building experience intended to better them as a Liege, that they had wanted to follow in the proud traditions of their father before them. Some appropriate lies that would have sounded good. When it came up in conversation, as it inevitably would have, they would have made polite chit chat until, eventually, people would stop bringing it up and Nat would slip all the way back into their old patterns.

But Nat had been captured by pirates. And that complicated matters.

Lord Adelhard didn't sit in the chair behind his huge desk the way he had when he sent Nat away. Instead, he hovered close to the door, as if he wasn't quite sure what to do with himself.

Nat closed the door behind them, taking the time to breathe and squeeze the brass doorknob to ground themself into reality. All it served to do was remind them of leaving this room the last time, knowing their life would never manage to return, fully, to what it had been.

"Hello, father." They leaned against the wall, hip cocked, arms folded in front of them. A barrier. Protection. Holding themself together.

This was the man who had sent them to sea. Who had set them up for so many awful things to happen in doing so. They should have been angry, enraged, and completely walled off from him and his opinions and judgement. Nat could command an entire pirate crew. Could destroy a naval officer's confidence so thoroughly with their words that he couldn't physically fight them. Could verbally spar with Pirate Lord Tao. Could keep their family name secret from an entire world of pirates, at least for a good while. But when faced by their own father, the man who ruined their life, Nat might as well have been eight years old all over again and being taught that children do not talk back to their father. Not even in support of someone else.

It didn't matter that Lord Adelhard in his current state —hair greyer than ever, shoulders hunching slightly with age, at an obvious loss— was far less intimidating than any pirate Nat had so far faced. Their heart thundered in their chest. The sleeves of their shirt were damp with sweat from their palms. Their dandified smile wanted to melt away.

"Why are you here?" he asked again.

"I already told you that."

"Why have you come back?"

"Because I was invited to the wedding."

"How?"

"The same way as many others, I presume. Through the postal service."

"How? I don't—" He huffed out a hulking breath and wandered over to his desk. He picked up and pen and set it back down. "Mr Awthorn disappeared at the same time as you and was ransomed. We heard *nothing* about you. We thought..."

Awthorn had made it? Nat almost believed he would have died from his injuries before he ever made it back home. "Clearly I am here."

Lord Adelhard turned to face them again.

Nat gripped themself tighter.

"What happened on that ship?"

Nat tilted their head.

"What happened to you on *The Valiant?*"

Nat didn't flinch at the name, but Lord Adelhard reached out a hand anyway. Nat dodged away. "Your wife has made it quite clear that I am to keep out of the way. I shall endeavour to avoid doing further damage to our family's reputation."

"I thought you were dead." The words came out uncomfortably neutral. Impossible to read. Less information even than Tao with a secret he didn't want to share. Had Lord Adelhard hoped as much? Did he feel guilty about sending Nat away?

"And yet," they said. "I stand in your office."

*T*he docks bustled with activity, as all docks always did. People everywhere running errands, carting cargo, and dashing about like pirates with the navy on their tails. Plain, simple clothes in muted blues, greys, and browns filled the area. No bright blue and crisp white of naval officers.

Nat adjusted their waistcoat. It still didn't fit. Neither did the coat overlaying it, pressing down on their shoulders like the weight of waves pushing them under.

When Nat had first come through these docks, they had been a terrified young Liege thrown out of their home. People had jostled them from every direction as they tearfully searched out a ship. High society elegance hadn't easily translated to working port elegance. In a mirror of the way Bear and Aleksei had struggled to move across the ballroom the previous night.

Nat tried to shake off the past, but every time the weight of their coat prevented ease of movement, or the tightness of their waistcoat squashed the breath from their lungs, it put the physical memory of that small bag of their belongings hanging heavily on their shoulder, that feeling of rising panic at what a naval ship might be like, especially for a Liege and a dandy.

Mercy's Myth blended in with the merchant ships at the port, Hui only adding to that image with the way she waited at the base of the boarding plank. She suited a merchant port, leaning against a crate, her eyes tracking over the people passing by. But, then, Nat had stolen her from a merchant ship. She has just been so... unhappy there.

Nat paused where they stood, watching the ship. Watching Hui. Should they go back? Or should they just find a tailor and buy new clothes and never return to the ship or to sea at all?

Hui's eyes landed on them and she smiled.

Nat strode forward, offered her a brief greeting, and headed up the boarding plank straight into the captain's cabin. First things first: find clothes that fit.

Nat's wardrobe on *Mercy's Myth* was a riot of colour. Or, at least, they had thought it was. Now that they looked again, having already discarded the ill-fitting jacket and waistcoat to a pile on the floor, and half-way out of their shirt —they could rival Aleksei's usual state of unbuttoned-ness— they were starting to realise it... wasn't. There were plentiful colours, a variety of hues carefully arranged into outfit clusters. But everything melded. A theme presented itself. And that theme was... "Tao." It came out as a sigh.

They shook off thoughts of the Pirate Lord practically synonymous with green and gold. Tried to ignore the way all but a very select few outfits in their collection had green or gold elements. Tried to ignore the fact that those that didn't would still fit seamlessly into Tao's colour scheme.

Once suitably attired in a cobalt, indigo, and fawn ensemble that was, perhaps, a little bold for daytime wear in high society and for which Nat had no matching hat —hats blew away far too easily on a ship, at least the type of hats Nat would lean toward— they pulled open the door to the captain's cabin and started searching for bags. A trunk would be impossible to procure on a ship like this, not to mention Nat had no staff to carry it for them, so bags would have to do.

That same canvas and leather cross-body bag Aleksei had brought medical supplies down to the cells with lay crumpled in one of the cupboards. Nat grabbed it, trying not to think about the last time they had seen it even as their left arm itched as if it was still healing. Maybe it was. Tao would know.

But Nat wasn't thinking about him. They shook out anything left in the bag, letting it clatter to the floor of the cupboard without a second glance and retreated to the captain's cabin to attempt to pack some decent clothes.

The boarding plank rattled with footsteps. Nat poked their head out of the cabin.

All that careful attention to Aleksei's hair had been undone, returning to its typical unkempt look, seemingly extra messy compared to usual. As if someone other than Aleksei had been running hands through it. His waistcoat hung open over a poorly buttoned shirt. Nat's fingers twitched to yank the cravat, so carelessly stuffed in his pocket into their own hands and possibly choke him with it. When one borrowed clothes, one was supposed to take some kind of care about it.

"And where have you been?" they called.

Aleksei stopped short with a wince.

"Quite the walk of shame," Kajal snickered, hanging from the rigging like an oddly shaped spider, as usual.

Aleksei let himself in through the open captain's cabin door, closing the door behind him as he had so many times before.

To his credit, he pulled the cravat and pin out of his pocket. To his detriment, he shoved them into a heaped pile on the desk. He yanked off the jacket and waistcoat, adding them to the pile before attempting to roll his shoulders in the stylishly tight shirt. He dragged at the collar, unbuttoning the top few buttons.

"Sunflower!" Nat snapped. "Please explain why exactly you're undressing in the privacy of a closed cabin? Did you get a tattoo? A new scar?" They couldn't help but brush down their own upper arm where distinct lines of scars dipped into their flesh.

Aleksei's face dropped.

Nat tugged their hand away. They didn't need to remind Aleksei of that day, intentionally or otherwise.

"No," he said. "Sorry. I just— I can't stand these clothes!"

Nat hopped up to sit on the desk next to Aleksei's discarded clothing. "You're the one who insisted on accompanying me last night." And Nat still wasn't exactly sure why.

"Discomfort is temporary."

"Okay, if you're just looking to swap outfits, wouldn't *your* cabin be the better choice?"

"Victor invited me to the library."

Victor? Lord Roydon. Nat's fingers clenched on the desk edge as they tried to make a non-committal, non-judgemental noise.

Libraries were... particular spaces. To the vast majority of high society, a library was a quiet room filled with books, knowledge, and comfortable chairs. It was a receiving room for those who didn't fit in a parlour or study, a perfect meld of the two. For a dandy, however, a library could be so much else.

For a dandy to invite someone to a library during a ball, particularly when that ball was not hosted by their own family, allowed few possibilities. Either, one was being invited for indiscreet activities, or one was being invited to share sensitive information. In Nat's experience, more often than not, it had been both at once.

"Did you and Lord Roydon... find pleasure in my library?" Nat squeaked. It was one thing to be okay with pirates and the ease with which they apparently enjoyed such intimacies. But in Nat's receiving library!

"What? No. We," Aleksei paused and rolled his eyes, "Found pleasure in his flat later."

The breath whooshed out of Nat.

"In the library, he told me he knew I wasn't a real gentleman."

And there was that tension again. "And you went home with him anyway? How did he know?"

"Apparently he visited Kovia and saw no mention of the Zima family."

"Kovia is a big country."

"Either way."

"You admitted."

"He thinks I have duped you into believing I have a title in Kovia — he knows you don't speak the language."

"We used to be..." Nat searched for the appropriate word. "Allies."

"He promised to keep my secret." Aleksei trailed off, refusing to meet Nat's eye.

"Please tell me he didn't blackmail you into letting him into your pants."

"No. He tried to blackmail me for information about you."

Nat frowned. "Me?"

"Where have you been? How did we meet? What are your plans now that you're here? Do you have intention to stay?"

Ah. That sounded more like Lord Roydon. He was always more invested in information than anything else. He liked playing with people like they were bugs and he was a cat, blocking their routes and occasionally batting them around before finally destroying them or letting them go. Nat had used to find it intriguing. Had used to idolise the way he did it. They had never thought to be a bug. "What did you tell him?"

"That we met after you were relieved of duty on the navy ship. That you had intention to visit family. At which point he invited me to retire from the ball." A soft smile spread over his face. "We had breakfast together."

"You're going to see him again." The words came out a whisper. Not a question but a statement. Of course he would. Anyone who could make Aleksei smile like that was well worth his time.

For the time Nat had been on the ship, Aleksei had been their steadfast companion. They had their brief beginning, a few rushed kisses, all interrupted. It hadn't led anywhere and Nat regretted none of it. Not the kisses, nor the friendship gained out of it. Aleksei had been mooning over Tao for longer than Nat knew; it was nice to see him moving on. And it wasn't like Nat misunderstood how pirates viewed things like sex and pleasure. But something about this had their stomach twisting.

Because it was Roydon? A lord and a dandy?

"It is a distinct possibility," Aleksei answered.

Nat cleared their throat. Keep neutral. Don't ruin this for him. Aleksei is loyal to a fault. Don't ruin this. "Be careful."

"Careful?"

"He's a dandy. Anything you say to him, no matter when, will be parsed for subtext. He will use what you give him in any way he likes and he already knows you're masquerading as a gentleman."

"This is a dandy thing?"

"Yup."

"You do this too?"

Nat hesitated. "Yes. Sometimes."

Aleksei's face remained carefully neutral.

"What I'm trying to say is that we have an entire crew to protect here, regardless of your romantic ideals. As your captain, I'm *asking* you to keep them safe."

"Romantic ideals?" It came out clipped, accent heavy.

"You and he had breakfast. You intend to see him again— presumably in the same capacity. If this is not romance then I have been misled at several points."

"Not every pirate wants to live life like Tao, you know!"

"What does that mean?"

"Some of us want to find people. Connect with people. Pleasure isn't just sex, Nat."

"That's exactly my point! You and Roydon aren't just sharing— Romance is the thing that isn't—" How had a single night in high society so damaged Nat's ability to speak on such things. But they were right, weren't they? Romance was the thing that wasn't sex? Romance was the thing Nat had never, probably would never experience. It was the thing they weren't sure they had the capacity for, or at the very least not the time.

"And you are what?" Aleksei snapped. "Warning me off?"

"That's not what I'm doing."

"You let Tao tell you how it is to be a pirate and you took him at his word as if it was all absolutes. Is it just because you like him? Or are you as cold-hearted as he is?"

"That's not fair."

"You're so desperately scared of letting people in, even a little, that you can't handle the thought that someone else might want that. Might even be able to find it."

"I know Roydon! I've known him since I was twenty years old. I know what he's like and how he works. I'm not saying that there is no possibility that you two might share something special but do you really want to risk your entire crew for that? For what will, inevitably, have to come to an end? Unless you're planning on ceasing your pirate life and shacking up with him?"

Aleksei's jaw was as tight as it had been that first day they had met, when his previous captain had cut a man's throat for not making a choice in a timely enough manner.

Nat pressed their hands against their eyes. "I'm not trying to—"

"You might not be trying!" Aleksei snapped. "But you are doing! You are ruining!"

The word hit with more force than it should have. Ruining, ruinous, ruiner, ruined. How many times had those words been tossed at Nat? At people like them.

Aleksei stormed from the cabin, his discarded pile of clothes remaining on the desk with Nat.

13
It Is My Decision

Nat slung the bag into a random corner of the receiving library at Adelhard Manor. Shelves of leather-bound books covered almost every wall, only the one with the bay window stood bare of all shelves. Many a time, Nat had sat on that windowsill to stare down the Adelhard driveway.

A windowsill was no appropriate place to sit, but the second Lady Adelhard had filled it with plush pillows, supposedly decorative in nature, after she had spotted Nat perched on the hard wooden sill.

Nat pulled open the cupboard hidden behind the entry door, smiling when they found it still stuffed full of the second Lady Adelhard's penny dreadfuls and paperback novellas. Perhaps they should take one back for Aleksei. Or Tao. If they even went back at all.

Nat's favourite chair had been replaced by a much less comfortable looking set of receiving furniture. Did they used to be in the parlour? Nat couldn't blame Lady Adelhard for changing things up, leaving unused, unchanged rooms only invited gnomes and other such critters in and once you had gnomes...

At least that appeared to be the entirety of the changes made in Nat's old sanctuary.

They ran gentle fingertips along the spines of the books. This was always meant to be Nat's place: where they received their guests, where they conducted any business, where they could be trusted to be found. It had even been the location of most of their lessons.

This was the place they had laughed over tea with Lord Roydon; learnt the best ways to pretend a faint from Lady Bakshi after enthusing about her newest inventions; shared books and cake and subtly snide comments with Liege Mishra.

But now Roydon was hopelessly intertwined with Aleksei in complex ways Nat wasn't fully prepared to process. Now, Lady Bakshi was married. And Liege Mishra... maybe Nat could hope for the best there.

They sank into one of the new armchairs, springing back out immediately at the discomfort of it. "Perfect..."

They wandered over to the bureau stuffed in the corner halfway behind the curtains. They tugged down the desk and grabbed paper, a dip pen, inkwell, and leaning pad before curling up in the bay windowsill, tucked out of sight behind the curtains.

Step one: practise penmanship while coming up with potential ideas. Nat hadn't used a dip pen since being sent to sea, pencils were the writing tool of preference there, but it wouldn't do to send out high society notes in pencil. Nor would it do to have poor handwriting. If Nat had any hope of rebuilding some sort of network, they would need to start sending out cards.

"*You* didn't attend dinner at the Randalbury estate with us last night," Lady Adelhard accused over the mostly empty breakfast table.

"I didn't think it appropriate to attend a dinner I wasn't invited to."

"You, as you are so fond of telling me, are an Adelhard, which means you were invited."

"My return was a surprise. I didn't wish to pressure the Randalburys into feeding an extra person."

Lady Adelhard's mouth twisted.

Wrong angle. Of course the Randalburys could afford to feed Nat alongside the other Adelhards. "Nor to set a place," Nat continued. "As you have told me time and again, it can be a challenge to fit a Liege into a seating plan since it makes the numbers uneven."

That was a bald faced lie on the part of Lady Adelhard. The typical order of seating for any dinner had gentlemen and ladies lined up like squares on a chessboard. Lieges were to sit between them. If in doubt, or struggling to match numbers at all, seat a liege on the end of a table nearest either member of the hosting pair.

Lady Adelhard placed both hands on her bread plate and shifted it a little to the left, as if correcting its position. "You agreed," she began, not looking up from her place setting, "At Carrolline's engagement ball, that you would bring no harm to my daughter."

Technically that wasn't true, but Nat was in no mood to argue with Lady Adelhard before breakfast even began. "You requested that I stay away from her. I am holding to that."

"You must attend events with us."

The order had Nat's spine prickling, but they shrugged one shoulder in assent.

Lady Adelhard's nostrils flared.

Before anything more could be said, the breakfast room door squealed open to reveal Lord Adelhard, Carrolline trailing in his wake.

Breakfast passed with relative ease until Nat attempted to head out only to find themself caught by the arm.

"You will need to change your attire to receive with us this afternoon," Lady Adelhard demanded.

Nat stared at the hand on their arm until Lady Adelhard retracted it. They inclined their head and moved toward the stairs. Receiving with Lady Adelhard. What joy.

To Nat's mind 'changing their attire' did not necessitate a bath, but Lady Adelhard had one prepared for them anyway. The warm water released scented oil into a cloud around Nat, lingering in their hair even if they decided not to wash it— why would they, though? Getting the salt-roughness out of it would be nothing but relief.

But apart from cleaning their salty hair, Nat was dreading each piece of the bathing experience. Dysphoria always *always* appeared when Nat had nothing else to occupy their thoughts but the actuality of their body, naked at that, and having to make it clean. They tried to stave it off with the pleasantries of oils and foam and other ridiculous and unnecessary bath products but they could only do so much.

Scrunching up their nose, Nat sighed and reached for the soap. Rose scented. Ew. They did not want to smell like their step-mother. They put it back down. Everything on the ship was washed with the same citrus peel soap made aboard. Bedding to bodies always delightfully fresh and orangey. They should have brought some from the ship.

The scars along their left arm called for their attention. The texture somehow always a surprise, even now.

Dressing their newly-cleaned self in a sensibly ostentatious afternoon ensemble — yet more green— they squeezed the water from their hair with a spare clean shirt. It wasn't their usual choice but it certainly did the job nicer than a standard bath towel.

Nat sighed, tucking their cravat into their waistcoat, only to pull it out when it didn't sit flat. They retied it, but the problem persisted. Their hands fisted in the fabric. The urge to tear it washed through them.

Why did high society types have to change outfits so often anyway? It was annoying at best and a real time suck at worst. And if Nat could have just kept their breakfast outfit on then none of this would be happening with their hair wet and dangling in their face and a cravat that wouldn't sit properly!

They took a deep breath, resolving to try again. When it still would not lie flat, Nat yanked it off their neck. Their fingers bit into the fabric before hurling it toward the bed, ignoring the way it landed.

Tears prickled their eyes.

Why was everything so horrible here? Why was it not easy to just slip back into who they had been before? It wasn't like Nat had decided they were never going back to *Mercy's Myth* but should it not have been easier to stay?

They gripped their hair tightly in their hands, tugging just enough that pain spiked across their scalp, followed by the cool chase of water. They didn't need a cravat, right? They could pick something else. Nat wasn't a gentleman; they didn't need to abide by gentlemen's clothing standards. And yet, the idea of presenting themself in society with nothing decoratively wrapped around their neck pressed against Nat in the same way dysphoria did. They hardly wore cravats at all on the ship. But that was a pirate ship and this was decidedly not.

They poked their head out of the bedroom door. Lady Adelhard's overworked maid bustled out of Carrolline's room.

"Excuse me?" Nat called quietly.

The mousy woman flinched.

"I know you're busy," Nat offered. "But is there any chance you can help me with my cravat?"

The maid scurried into Nat's room, took one look at the sad cravat hanging half off the mattress and pulled open Nat's wardrobe instead. "Non-binare, oui?"

"Yes."

She pulled something from the wardrobe and fiddle around Nat's throat. Their hands fisted at their sides.

Once she was done she disappeared as quickly as she had come, leaving Nat with the mirror alone again. A wide black ribbon sat under the collar of Nat's shirt. It crossed over itself near their top button, Nat's favourite cravat pin keeping it in place. Perfectly flat, perfectly gender neutral, perfectly unique.

Revitalised, Nat bounded down the stairs, ready to face whatever high society and the Adelhards wanted to throw at them this afternoon.

"I'm just saying, husband." Lady Adelhard's voice had Nat pausing on the stairs. "Encouraging your eldest offspring out of the house will only do good things. Both for us and for Carrolline."

"Carrolline is already engaged." Lord Adelhard at least had the decency to keep his voice down.

Nat sank into a sitting position, holding onto the banister rail as if it would protect them from what they were hearing.

"To a man I have yet to meet," Lady Adelhard snipped.

"It is my—"

"I am not disagreeing with your decision, husband." Her voice turned placating. "All I am saying is that... Nat is odd at the best of times, and since they got back from wherever they have been, they have become odder still."

"Oddness is no reason to kick someone out."

"I would never suggest kicking them out, this is their family home. I just think encouraging them to rent a flat might be wise. Our poor staff are already overworked without adding a dandy to the mix."

"Then you should have hired more competent people."

Once again Lady Adelhard's voice turned sharp. "Do you care at all for our reputation?"

"I have already spoken to... *them* about keeping a low profile." It stung to know Lord Adelhard couldn't even bring himself to say their name.

"You think that will change anything?" Lady Adelhard scoffed. "Do you really want to wait for another incident like last time?"

"And you think letting them out of our sight is the solution to that?"

"You're the one who sent them away to begin with!"

"To the navy where their every move would be observed."

"But—"

"Enough, woman. It is my decision and I will think on it."

Nat pressed their forehead against the banister as Lord and Lady Adelhard's footsteps retreated.

Another incident like last time.

What had they expected? That their brief absence would heal the damage? That their family might have missed them? Might love them enough to move on?

No. Nobody in high society would ever think of Nat as anything other than their almost-scandal. And nobody in pirate society would ever think of Nat as anything other than their origins: a weak dandy prisoner who offered up sewing skills to keep themself alive.

14
Oh. Oh No.

fternoon receiving had been surprisingly painless. Lady Adelhard had only a few visitors, allowing Nat to sit quietly in the most comfortable armchair in the room, right next to the fireplace.

They changed, once again, into a beautiful red and gold swirled outfit, swapping their favourite cravat pin for a more suitable gold one but maintaining the ribbon tie rather than trying again with the cravat proper. They hadn't often been wearing cravats since leaving the only one they'd had on the bed with Tao when they had stormed out. They'd bought a few but every time they stood aboard *Mercy's Myth* and pulled that fabric around their throat it filled them with that feeling of Tao's clever fingers undoing the knot, whipping the fabric from around their neck, tying their wrists with it.

If the carriage ride to dinner had any conversation, Nat was oblivious to it. They leaned heavily against the carriage wall, arms wrapped around their stomach as if it would hold them together. Their face felt hot, as if they were flushed even in the relative cool of the evening air seeping through gaps in the carriage door.

Carrolline ducked her head close to Nat's as a house large enough to rival Adelhard Manor appeared in view of the windows. "I am glad you're coming," she whispered.

Nat tried to smile.

"Lady Georgiana Isaksen hates me because I look so much finer in pearls than she." Carrolline touched a hand to the string of pearls around her neck.

Now that she mentioned it, she was wearing an awful lot of pearls. Pearls stitched into the bodice of her gown, woven into her updo making her hair seem all the darker, and even pearl buttons at the edges of her gloves. Perhaps she was more like her mother than Nat expected with that level of opulence.

Disembarking the carriage, Carrolline leaned in to whisper, "There's Georgi—I mean, Lady Isaksen. Let's go!"

Nat attempted to make pleasant conversation with the young Lady Georgiana Isaksen, who appeared to be

Carrolline's age and the third apparent child of the Isaksen family.

When Carrolline began tossing her head at the young lady as they all stepped into the parlour, Nat excused themself to talk with the other Isaksens. Watching Carrolline flirting was definitely too much to handle on this particular day.

The dining room was an opulent space filled with more rich colours than one typically wanted to see when eating. Nat settled between Lord Albert Isaksen and his eldest sister, who didn't deign to give Nat either her first name, nor any of her attention.

Lord Albert Isaksen seemed a pleasant enough fellow. He had a round face that reminded Nat of some of the stylised paintings from Tao's palace. Which set a wash of surprising adrenaline blasting out from Nat's heart like a firework.

His outfit had been meticulously put together in a way that appealed to Nat's dandy sensibilities. They even matched one another in colour — although Lord Isaksen's plain red waistcoat with golden buttons and edging was nowhere near as extravagant as the delicate patterning coating Nat's entire waistcoat, jacket and trousers.

On occasion, he turned from his conversations with the elder Adelhards to attempt to invite Nat to join them. Nat responded politely to his questions, grateful that it didn't take long for the conversation to pass away.

The residual unpleasantness in their chest prevented enough air from entering their lungs to engage in full conversation. It sent the clever parts of Nat's brain scattering away from them like rats in the light.

When dinner was over, the elder Lord Isaksen invited the gentlemen to retire to his smoking room for brandy. Nat stood, abandoned in the hallway as the party split by gender, gentlemen following Lord Isaksen and ladies trailing into the parlour with his wife.

They leaned their head back against the wall. Would it be so bad to leave quietly? They could simply walk back to Adelhard Manor. It would take time, but Nat wasn't exactly pressed for that.

"There you are," Lord Albert Isaksen said, emerging from the door through which the gentlemen had disappeared. "I realised my father had made a small blunder. I suppose we're all used to it just being your parents and your sister."

Nat pushed off the wall and offered an attempt at a smile.

"Would you care to tour the grounds?"

"Sure," Nat agreed. They followed Lord Isaksen out of a back door and into a well-lit garden so much like the Adelhard promenading garden that it might as well have been transported there.

"If I may be so forward..."

Nat gripped their shirt cuffs. Here it was. The reminder. The question. The expectation.

"I get the impression you don't want to be here tonight?"

Nat watched the way their footsteps and Lord Isaksen's matched up. Left then right. They would be terrible together in a three-legged race. Not that any adult would participate in such a thing. "A minor disagreement," Nat lied easily.

This was nothing like walking up to Tao's palace, the Pirate Lord's arm wrapped in theirs, tugging them along. And yet, Nat was just as trapped here as they had been back then.

"About?"

They smiled at Lord Isaksen. "Do you make such personal enquiries to everyone upon your first meeting?"

He laughed. A pleasant sound. It tilted his chin up, revealing a soft scar just on its underside.

"A question for a question, then?" Nat suggested. "The scar on your chin?"

His smile was just as soft as the rest of him. No secret under-layers, no danger, just kindness. "I fell over as a child."

"That's it?"

He shrugged. "That's it. On the tiled floor of a train station."

"Adventurous traveller?"

"Visiting my grandparents in Orksure."

"My return wasn't exactly as well planned as it should have been," Nat finally answered the question Lord Isaksen had posed. "I suppose such is the risk of sea travel."

"You've been at sea?"

"*How* do you feel about your not-yet-twenty year-old daughter marrying?" Nat asked.

The chairs in dressmakers shop weren't comfortable, but at least they were there. Lady Adelhard sat in the one opposite Nat in the viewing section of the shop, a back room away from the front where people could book appointments. Carrolline was back in the dressing room with the dressmaker herself, being buttoned into whatever it was that they were here for.

On another day, Nat might had tried to get out of attending the fitting, but the way Carrolline had looked at them and said, "Having another pair of eyes can only be helpful. And you know so much of fashion — mama, Nat was the one who reminded me ruffles are going out of style."

Lady Adelhard hadn't argued then, but she also hadn't acknowledged Nat the entire way to town, nor since.

"My feelings are none of your concern," she said, voice cold.

Nat held their hands up in surrender. "Just thought I'd check on your emotional well-being. Excuse me for presuming your husband has been neglecting that a little."

"My emotional well-being is none of your concern," she repeated.

Nat slumped in the chair. "Have it your way."

"You brought this upon yourself," Lady Adelhard hissed, eyes darting around to ensure they were alone.

"Because I've been gone?"

"Something a little more damning than your absence."

The insult hit like a bop on the nose from an unsecured sail, a pain that came with the shame of having done a poor job.

"Sit up straight, for goodness sake."

Nat straightened their spine, small cracks and pops accompanying the movement.

In the light streaming through the frosted windows, Carrolline emerged. The gown clung to her like a glove, the silk of the bodice shining, lending an air of gold to Carrolline. Beads and gems glittered across the neckline and at the edges of the sleeves. The skirt flared in accordance with fashion, lace leading lines around each gathered layer.

"Just picture it with gloves and your veil," Lady Adelhard gushed, hands fluttering over her daughter's hands and hair.

Carrolline faced herself in the mirror, lips pulled into a smile that didn't touch the rest of her. A portrait of a smile.

She smoothed her hands down her front. Again that movement that Nat was acutely and uncomfortably familiar with.

With almost no tweaks left to be made, the seamstress lead Carrolline back into the dressing room, leaving Nat and Lady Adelhard where they sat once again.

"I expect you to present your intended receiving outfiture for approval once we return home."

Home. What a joke.

*N*at's choice of a bright forest green and pastel blue ensemble —another one that would appeal to Tao— seemed to pass Lady Adelhard's inspection.

She accompanied Nat downstairs and into the parlour. It had been laid out perfectly to encourage conversation. Two long sofas faced one another, one on the entry wall and one with its back to the window. On the fireplace side of the room sat a pair of armchairs for the more unsociable sort and opposite them one short sofa barely appropriate for two and another singular armchair. Tucked away in the corner sat

Carrolline's piano which Nat could be certain had so many layers of dust inside it that it wouldn't sound a single note.

Nat moved toward their usual choice of the armchair by the fireplace that faced the window. But Lady Adelhard's hand on their arm stopped them. It touched at the scars decorating Nat's skin, making them shiver. She deposited them on the smaller sofa directly opposite their usual choice.

Carrolline stepped through the door in a violet gown with a rounded skirt and triangular neckline that matched on the front and the back. Lady Adelhard arranged her on one of the larger sofas, taking her own seat on the opposite one.

Did she always organise things so thoroughly? She hadn't been this particular with Nat unless they were hosting the young lady or lord she was pushing Nat to favour. But Carrolline was already engaged, so that couldn't be it.

And anyway, she would have put Carrolline on the small sofa. She claimed it fostered intimacy to sit that close with a potential partner.

Oh.

Oh no.

No, no no.

Nat surged to their feet, legs tensed to flee, but even as they did so, the parlour door opened and a contingent of visitors appeared.

"Lord Isaksen," Lady Adelhard greeted. "I'm sure you remember Liege Adelhard and, of course, my daughter."

Between the way Lord Isaksen's — Alfred? Alison? Albert? Albert! — cravat was tied, the laziest knot Nat had ever had the misfortune to witness, and the slightly too showy waistcoat, Nat's desire to flee only increased. He was dressed up nicer than expected for tea.

Carrolline stood long enough to curtsy. She shared a long look with the younger Isaksen, who promptly shifted over to sit with her on the larger sofa, immediately dipping into low, private conversation. No help there, then.

"Liege Adelhard," Lord Isaksen greeted, holding out a hand.

Did he want to shake? Was he intending to kiss Nat's hand? Wouldn't that be a telling choice. Nat ignored it, shot a glare at Lady Adelhard, and slammed back down on the smaller sofa.

Lord Isaksen took the seat next to them.

Yup. This was definitely a set up. And Nat had fallen for it.

Fuck.

"You were telling me about your adventures at sea," he invited.

"Yes," Lady Adelhard interjected. "Nat had been visiting extended family across the sea." Maybe she would insert herself so thoroughly into the conversation that Nat wouldn't actually have to say anything at all.

"Where abouts?"

Nat's fingers rubbed back and forth on the forest green silk of their jacket. Had this been a gift from Tao? He had offered a whole parcel-full after the carousel conversation with the note '*To a wonderful friendship or a terrible rivalry*'. Nat had been too peeved to open it until they had left the port.

"East." Nat's voice left them in a soft breath.

"I always longed to travel." Lord Isaksen's knees had turned toward Nat.

Lady Adelhard dipped out to pretend to chase up the tea. Just like she had insisted on disappearing with one of the other attempts' chaperone to show off her prised roses—not that Lady Adelhard tended to garden nor cared about roses.

"There's nothing like it," Nat said. "Wind in your hair, salt spray on your skin."

"Surely you can't enjoy the sailing so much?" He pressed the back of a hand delicately to his lips, as if nauseated. "All those sailors shouting and barrelling about? I was under the impression you didn't currently hold a naval position."

Barrelling about seemed a chaotic view of the perfected mechanics of the crew on *Mercy's Myth*. From the first moment Nat had been permitted onto the deck they had seen the intricate movement for what it was: a dance where all parties knew exactly what steps to take. Kajal like a spider in the rigging. Jay joking as xe moved around the ship. Bear, a sturdy presence, always on the lookout. Aleksei supervising as he flowed across the ship like a river around rocks. Sometimes, even now, Nat stood at the rear of the ship and just watched them all work.

Nat closed their hand, realising they were tracing the lines of the tattoo decorating their inner forearm over their silk jacket. "I think if a crew is organised enough, it looks more like dancing than barrelling."

"To each their own."

"Indeed." Nat took a breath, letting the relative silence settle before nodding toward Carrolline and Georgiana. "Our sisters seem to be getting along particularly well."

"To think that Georgiana was just boasting that the young Lady Adelhard would think she too prim in her high necked gown. It doesn't seem to be bothering her at all. She will surely miss your sister upon her marriage."

"Indeed."

"Regarding the marriage, what do you know of the suitor in question?"

Nat's eyebrows drew together. Did even Lord Isaksen, an apparently highly regarded member of society —even if Nat had no previous memory of him— also have no information to share on Carrolline's fiancé? Who was this man? What was Lord Adelhard thinking?

More urgently, how in the world was Nat to answer a question like that? And could they truly offer Carrolline the help she had requested without that information?

"I have only just returned," they said. An avoidance.

"I was given to understand he was a naval man, I just thought you might have known him from your travels."

"I think we travel in different circles."

15
Lost At Sea

Time seemed to stretch between endlessness and nothingness. Lady Adelhard did not let Nat go, would not allow them any time alone, any time to chance a visit to the ship.

The more that endless-nothingness time built up, the more guilt ate at Nat.

A ball fluttered on around them. All swirls of colour and laughter and so much perfume that it made Nat dizzy. They took up refuge by the open garden doors, the fresh evening air clearing their head and their lungs.

A red and gold whirlwind of a person appeared to Nat's right hand side. They turned a smile to Liege Mishra.

Xyr hair had been pulled into a utilitarian bun atop xyr head, except for the dyed red and gold feathers clipped to drape down like a veil that brushed at xyr neck.

"Liege Mishra," Nat greeted.

Liege Mishra hmm'd noncommittally.

"How have you been?"

"Fine." Xe wouldn't look at Nat.

"Jothi?"

"I would expect you not to address me so informally."

"What?"

"We aren't friends anymore, Liege Adelhard," Liege Mishra hissed, perfect practised smile not shifting with the venom in xyr voice.

Nat swallowed.

"I hate to say it so bluntly but you leave me no choice." Xyr voice cut into Nat like a thousand perfectly aimed hat pins. "You disappear without even a goodbye, and suddenly you come back and expect everyone to be okay with that? We thought you were dead! Were you aware of that? Your family acted as though you had been lost at sea and we all know lost at sea is code for dead."

"I was lost at sea," Nat whispered.

"I don't care. I did my mourning. I'm done. You may not be dead but you're dead to me. Stop sending cards."

The lump of tears surged up Nat's throat. They swallowed tightly and nodded once. They couldn't pull the dandy persona around themself, they couldn't even manage their neutral captain's face.

Liege Mishra strode away. Nat watched the way xyr coattails swished with the movement.

Lady Bakshi's parlour rug was not the same. Unsurprising since this wasn't the same parlour. Nor was she, technically, Lady Bakshi any longer. The previous purple and green peacock rug had been tossed in favour of an intricate but meaningless pattern of varying shades of blue and green. The furniture matched it so well that it must, also, be new with the house and the name and the husband.

Creams, turquoises, and blues decorated the walls and soft furnishings. Pale wooden tables, shelves, and sofa legs contrasted with Nat's expectations so starkly that they had to take a few breaths before they could find a seat.

Pirates really did seem to favour dark woods. Maybe it was just Tao, though. Nat had spent more time with him, in his spaces, than anyone or anywhere else but the ship itself.

Uneven spaces between the delicate sandwiches on the tea set atop the table in the centre of the seating area told that Lady Bakshi had received more than just Nat so far this afternoon. It was common practise to see several people within any given afternoon, just because a summons from Tao meant Tao's full attention didn't relate to high society. And why was Nat trying to compare the two things anyway? They were fundamentally different experiences.

But Nat had got that calling card inviting them to visit with Rajni. They had traced the perfectly penned letters with their fingertips, followed the swirl of their name and the R in place of Rajni. They had debated with Lady Adelhard whether it would be appropriate to go alone, having to utilise Lady Bakshi's marital name and status as a tool in their arsenal. Eventually they'd decided to just slip out the back door when Lady Adelhard wasn't looking and walk all the way to the address listed on the calling card.

Lady Bakshi's afternoon receiving garb took no influence from Endrish fashions; she wore a blue, turquoise and silver sari that matched perfectly with the room's colour scheme. She served tea into a pair of clean cups that also matched her outfit and the room: delicate silver and turquoise designs exploring the surface of the porcelain.

"You're awfully quiet for a woman who invited me over," Nat supplied when it became clear that Lady Bakshi wasn't going to say anything.

She raised an eyebrow.

"You're angry with me." Just like her sibling-in-law at the ball the previous night.

The calling card itself had been sparse on the detail and more plain in style than Nat was used to from Lady Bakshi. The lack of extra information hiding within the card itself was very telling. Nat had examined the word choice for a synonym-based secret message, explored the pattern running around the cards edge for hidden words, and yet they had found nothing.

It would have been easy enough to shrug off, except for Nat and Rajni's history.

"You're behaving strangely," Lady Bakshi accused in that gently lilting voice of hers, the movement of her mouth causing her cascading silver earrings to sway.

"A lot has happened," Nat hedged.

"You were lost at sea, I got married; it's not that much."

"I still can't believe you got married."

"You cannot be that uncomfortable with my marital status. You were gone, Nat. What else was I meant to do?"

"That's not what I—"

"We could have made the best of it, but no. You just disappeared!"

Nat looked down into their tea cup. Black tea. It seemed weird now. Drinking black tea in a delicate porcelain cup. Nat had somehow become used to tankards of black tea with too much sugar and no milk available. Delicate teacups were meant for jasmine tea and Tao's secret receiving room.

"You didn't even leave me a note," Rajni breathed.

"I didn't get the chance."

The smile she offered Nat was one Nat was uncomfortably, intimately familiar with. The same kind of smile Nat wrapped around themself when the pain pushing at them pressed a little too hard.

"You didn't tell me you were coming back either."

"I didn't," Nat agreed. And the real question was why. It hadn't even occurred to them. They had been so focused on having upset Tao.

But Rajni had once been the person to whom Nat compared all others. She was the one person in Nat's entire life that they had considered the possibility of falling in love with.

Looking at her now, she was just as beautiful, just as intelligent and witty. She hadn't changed – but for the name.

So what had?

The door to Adelhard Manor rattled as it opened. Nat had barely taken two steps inside when Lady Adelhard bustled out of the parlour, face twisted in a mask of rage. "Where have you been?" she hissed.

"Visiting with Lady Ba— Mishra."

"Lord Albert Isaksen is sat on the other side of that door. He arrived with the intention of courting you."

Nat snorted. "That's not going to happen."

Lady Adelhard's head reared back. "Excuse me?"

"I said that's not going to happen. For a start he should have sent a card, but more importantly I'm not going to be courted by Lord Albert Isaksen."

"And what makes you think you will find better than Lord Albert Isaksen?"

"It's not about better. If I agree to be—" Nat cut themself off with an expelled breath. Albert Isaksen was perfectly nice. In another world Nat might have considered him an ideal prospect. But for the fact that he was set to inherit his family's estate and Nat was also expected to do so for their own family.

He was soft and gentle. He liked the thought of travel but hated the idea of sail. He was kind enough to notice Nat had been left out but not so bold as to make a scene.

He paid attention to Nat. Asked them insightful questions. Listened intently. He had a soft face and a gentle easy laugh. He would be the kind of husband who had no qualms about Nat continuing their dandy tendencies —though Nat had always believed they would remain committed to someone they chose to marry, so certain dandy activities would be off the table purely for Nat's own sensibilities.

And all of that meant Albert Isaksen deserved someone who could love him back. And Nat would never be able to. They might have once, love could have grown from fondness but that was before. Before living over the sea. Before being submitted to the pain that lingered like an ill-healing bruise. Before learning how to dandy like a pirate. Now, such a life and such a bond would scrape at Nat like a poorly constructed chair, nails and splinters digging into their flesh. And it would do the same to whomever Nat was bound to. Maybe it always would have.

"Please convey my apologies to the Isaksens and, if you can, throw in a hint that I'm not marrying anyone let alone Albert Isaksen. Excuse me." They swept past Lady Adelhard and toward the receiving library.

16
Do I Look Any Straighter To You?

Lady Adelhard didn't bother to acknowledge Nat the next morning at breakfast, going so far as to chase the heels of her husband both into and out of the breakfast room.

Nat took themself off to hide in the library until the Adelhards were all ensconced in their afternoon activities. Lady Adelhard entertaining guests in the parlour and Lord Adelhard talking with a business partner in his study. The door to the parlour clunked shut and Nat poked their head out of the library to call softly for, "Brett?"

The ever-present butler emerged from his haunt.

"Could you arrange for the carriage to take me to town?"

Brett pressed his lips together.

Nat tilted their head.

"I feel it is my duty to inform you... though I doubt your father will appreciate my doing so. Nevertheless, I feel it is my duty to inform you that he has asked to be notified should I be aware of you leaving the house."

Nat's eyebrows drew together. "Why?"

"I believe he is..." Brett's eyes narrowed. "Concerned about the family reputation."

Nat pacified their face. "Thank you for letting me know, Brett. Belay the carriage request."

"Very good, My Liege." With that he disappeared back down the hallway.

Lord Adelhard wanted to be informed about Nat's every move. That was going to make things difficult. On the other hand...

Nat slunk out of the library and through the hall. They grabbed a top hat from the cloakroom — it was plain black and didn't quite match the pastels coating the rest of Nat's outfit but Nat could resolve themself to that.

Tentatively they pulled open the front door. They squished themself through the tiniest possible gap in the door, closing it behind them just as carefully. With the door closed, Nat hesitated a heartbeat longer. No roaring Adelhards.

They shot a furtive look at the parlour windows, if Lady Adelhard looked out now she'd see Nat taking off down the driveway. Not that Nat had much of a choice; there was no other way off Adelhard grounds. It would be fine; Lady Adelhard wouldn't look, not with guests.

Once they were hidden behind the outer wall they slowed down to a comfortable stroll. The walk was pleasant enough, late August sunlight shone warm and orange on the wild berry bushes opposite the estate.

The thudding of horses hooves on dirt tickled Nat's consciousness. They turned on the path to see what kind of vehicle approached.

The Adelhard family carriage pulled to a stop next to Nat. The door flung open and Lord Adelhard's splotchy red face peered out. "What in the world do you think you're doing?" He roared.

Had he left his business associate alone in his office? How had he known Nat had gone? Had Brett really told on them?

"Walking," they answered.

The way Lord Adelhard's eyes blazed told Nat that was the wrong answer. "Where?"

"Oh, you know," Nat circled a hand in the air, "here, there."

"Get in the carriage."

"I'm quite happy to walk."

"That was not a request."

"Oh? I'm sorry, Sir." Nat's voice dripped with sarcasm and disdain. "I hadn't realised you intended to treat your child as a subordinate officer. My mistake." They climbed slowly and with all the dandified elegance they could muster into the carriage.

Lord Adelhard slammed the door closed.

The silence stretched between them. Nat watched the world pass by the window. The road leading up to Adelhard manor was too narrow for a carriage to make a full turn, so the driver had to travel to where the road widened. The cross junction that lead either to town, to Lady Rajni's old house, or to the more populated area where the Roydon, Mishra, and Harcroft families lived. Nat closed their eyes, too pained to watch the return to Adelhard Manor.

"Did Brett tell you?" Lord Adelhard's quiet voice made Nat flinch.

"Tell me what?" They didn't bother turning to look at Lord Adelhard.

"Did Brett tell you to avoid using the carriage?"

"I couldn't have just wanted to walk?"

"In the early afternoon August sun? I may not know much about dandies but I do know you and your freckles and I do remember how self-conscious you were about gaining more."

Now Nat did turn to face him. "You think I wouldn't have got over that? There aren't many places to hide from the sun on a ship's deck. Why would Brett have warned me to avoid using the carriage?"

"So he wouldn't have to alert me to your use of it."

"You asked Brett to ground me." The contained rage made each word sharp, an embroidery needle repeatedly stabbing the same piece of fabric. "As if I am not a fully capable adult. As if I have not been supporting and maintaining myself. As if I were an unruly child."

"You can see why I felt it necessary," he mumbled.

"What exactly did you expect me to be doing on a weekday afternoon? Am I not permitted to visit with my friends? Attend appropriate social activities? Or is it merely that I must run all my actions past my commanding officer — oh, I'm sorry, I obviously mean my father — first?"

"Don't argue with me!" Lord Adelhard's voice exploded from him. "You brought this on yourself. Your clandestine activities—"

"Is that going to haunt the rest of my life?" Nat roared back. "I know high society has a long memory, I know the memory of what happened is in the back of enough people's minds that it wouldn't take much to dredge it back up. But Rajni is married now, I am hardly about to put that into question even if I wasn't painfully aware of the way that activities like that will affect the entire family. Most importantly Carrolline."

"It cannot be held to your activities from—" he cleared his throat "— before. You just snuck out of the house to go wherever you intended today! Yesterday too, you snuck out. I need to know where you're going and what you're doing."

"Perhaps if I were afforded a modicum of trust I wouldn't feel the need to sneak anywhere."

The carriage pulled to a stop in front of Adelhard Manor. Nat flung the door open before the footman could leap to their aid.

"Does your family mean nothing to you?" Lord Adelhard called after Nat, voice booming in the still summer air. It made Nat think of Tao's revelation, the way he had described the voice of the terrifying Admiral Adelhard.

Nat spun, a brittle laugh escaping them. "That's pretty rich for a man who banished his heir to sea."

"For a year!"

In the corner of Nat's eye, something shifted. People looking out the parlour window. This was not the place to have a conversation like this. Too public. But Lord Adelhard had started this and Nat wasn't just going to stand there and take it.

"I believe your exact words were 'a year at sea should straighten you out' — or am I mistaken?"

"What of it?"

"I was given to understand you meant, were I not 'straightened out' by the year's end, I would not be welcome to return." They flung their arms wide, presenting their fanciful clothing, their dandified stance only changed slightly by a year of piracy. "Do I look any straighter to you?"

Lord Adelhard deflated like a balloon that hit a sharp rock. "That isn't..."

"Isn't what? The case? Then why such a tight hold on the reins? Why the constant supervision. Not to mention the fact that your own wife told me to keep out of Carrolline's business, at best, the very first night of my return. You think I haven't heard you debating the best way to get rid of me since then? Give me a little credit. I am not a child and I am not oblivious. Now, if you're done playing politics with your own household and if you're done expecting me to treat you like a naval superior, I—"

The slap rang out, echoing in the subsequent silence.

Nat took a deep, even breath. Their hands fisted at their sides. "That was wholly unnecessary," they snarled.

Lord Adelhard's head reared back, causing his neck to bunch up under his chin.

The last time Lord Adelhard had slapped Nat, they had fallen to the floor with the force of it. Tears had streamed down their face, they had cradled their cheek, they had stuttered out an apology.

That had been before the navy ship.

Before being captured by pirates.

Before all the blood and pain that Nat had endured because of those experiences. Because of Lord Adelhard's decisions.

Nat's face burned with the blood rushing to it but they didn't reach up to touch it. Lord Adelhard could watch the way he turned his child's face as red as their hair. He could watch and he could feel whatever emotion might spark in his cold dark mind.

One more breath. One more frozen second. One last chance to salve the wound, to save the chance at a relationship.

Nat turned and entered the Manor.

17

You Seem Besieged By Those

Nat didn't bother to respond to the knock on the library door. Who cared for their privacy? Who ever had?

Brett poked his head around the door. "My Liege, a Lord Roydon to see you."

They unfolded themself from the windowsill. "Show him in please, Brett."

"Very good."

Nat slumped into one of the uncomfortable chairs that had replaced the set they had known and loved. They felt like sharp glass tossed into the sea, shifting from cutting to rough and scraping.

"Liege Adelhard," Lord Roydon's voice swept over Nat like the brush of fabric over the back of their neck. He paused just inside the door, eyes tracking over the red mark on Nat's slapped cheek. His practised smile didn't break, but it did freeze in place.

Brett brought in tea as Roydon picked his seat.

"I cannot thank you enough for introducing me to the lovely Mr Zima."

Nat searched for the intent behind the words, rough edges catching on any dip or edge and scraping against their insides. They swallowed and forced their own smile. It twinged on their bruise. "Yes, I hear you two have become quite close."

"Indeed we have. He is possessed of a unique set of attributes."

Nat nodded slowly, trying not to think too hard about which of Aleksei's particular attributes Lord Roydon was enjoying. "I'm sure you know he and I are friends."

"No offence, Hummingbird, but I doubt your friendship is much going to affect him here."

Hard as Nat clung to their persona, to the dandy presentation they had practised for as many years as they had been counted something like an adult, more years than they hadn't used it, it shattered. They surged into motion, serving the tea in the desperate, unbearable, and completely futile hope that it would prevent Roydon from noticing.

Roydon leaned forward but instead of taking the newly poured tea cup, he placed a hand over Nat's. They looked up at him, faces closer than propriety should allow. "Dearling, what in the world happened to your face?"

Nat couldn't stop their free hand from rising to touch at their face. It was hot. Their voice came out soft. "An unfortunate incident..."

"You seem to be besieged by those in this household."

"We don't pick the families we're born into."

"Indeed we don't." The words came out serious. Nothing like what Nat had heard from him before. He shifted to pick up the tea cup. That serious manner remained. "You're never going to tell anyone, are you?"

"Tell anyone what?"

"Anything relating to what transpired after you and Rajni got caught in that library. I asked Aleksei and he had no idea what I was talking about."

"We were caught outside the library, you need better intel."

"Apologies for misremembering a minor scandal from almost two years ago, wild-one."

"Forgiven," Nat teased with a soft smile.

"But I'm right."

"That I intend to keep my secrets secret? Yes."

Lord Roydon sighed. "A secret for a secret, at all tempting?"

"Depends on the secret. You can ask, and offer your secret as payment."

"Because then you can decree whether you'll answer the question at all and how much my own secret is worth?"

"Of course."

"You never could do things in a simple manner."

"Self-protection rarely is simple. Particularly for heirs." And pirate prisoners. And pirate captain's whose fathers were decorated naval admirals.

"I wouldn't know," Lord Roydon mused. He took his time thinking of his question.

"I'm not a genie; I won't twist your question."

That got a laugh. "I'm just musing over what I most want to know." Another pause and then, "Where have you been? Your current residence — not Adelhard Manor."

"I'll answer."

"My secret..." He thought again. "I really like Aleksei. More than I've ever liked anyone. If he were a real gentleman I would..."

He didn't need to finish. Lord Roydon would invite Aleksei to live with him in his bachelor pad. He would commit to Aleksei. The closest he, as a member of the ton, could get to marriage with another man.

Nat swallowed painfully. "I live on a ship."

Lord Roydon shifted to frown at them. "Not naval?" he gaped.

"Fuck no!"

Laughter burst out of Roydon. "Merchant then?"

Nat glanced at the door, it remained closed. They shook their head.

"If it's not a naval or a merchant vessel then what...?" he trailed off, mind whirling like a spinning top.

"What would you give up for him? For Aleksei?" Nat asked.

"More than I'm willing to admit. How did the two of you meet?"

Nat considered the question. "Someone tried to kill me."

"What? Aleksei did?"

"No. He was just... around when it happened."

"Stepped in like a dashing rescuer?"

Nat stared into their tea cup, remembering the white line of Aleksei's jaw as it stood out starkly with tension. Doing his best to cope with the captain he had and the way his loyalty to her warred with his own wants and needs. "That's not who he is."

"Oh?"

"But maybe it's different for you."

That evening, bedecked in bronze and surprisingly matching Carrolline's taffeta gown, Nat ended up sat in a painfully silent carriage as the whole Adelhard contingent headed out to a ball.

As the carriage pulled up the driveway to a manor-house far larger than the Adelhard home, Lord Adelhard leaned over to hiss in Nat's ear, "Do not embarrass me tonight."

As if the bright purple bruise on their face wouldn't do that all on its own.

Gas lamps had been lit all round the edges of the Great Hall, even as the evening sun shone through the huge windows all along the western wall. Pink, red, and white curtains had been gathered on either side of each window, matching the likely colour of the sunset when it came.

Carrolline touched a hand to Nat's arm. "Ask me to dance?"

Nat opened their mouth to refuse; they were hardly in the mind-set to subject themself to something so awful as dancing at a ball. But instead they forced a smile. "My Lady, Carrolline." They performed a nonbinary bow in the most over-dramatic fashion they could manage, eyes flicking away from Lord Adelhard's glare over the top of Carrolline's head. "If I might have the honour of a dance?"

Carrolline took Nat's proffered hand, bobbing into her own curtsy with a giggle before Nat led her onto the dance floor.

Thankfully it was a quartet piece, not a paired dance. The band began the music and Nat and Carrolline launched into motion, coming together and parting as the dance demanded.

"I heard you and father outside the house," Carrolline said. "Did mother really say that? About staying away from me?"

"It wasn't quite so clean as that."

"Is that why you've been avoiding me? — ow!" she complained as Nat's foot strayed too close and onto Carrolline's.

"I miss the days of huge hoop skirts," Nat moaned. "It was so much harder to step on a woman's feet then."

Carrolline laughed lightly, thoroughly distracted from her point. The dance demanded they join into quartets with a nearby couple and Nat stumbled again upon realising their new partner was Rajni, resplendent once again in a wonderful mesh of cultures and traditions. The long sleeves of a married woman's gown, paired with a turquoise sari covered in white stars and with a band of gold along one edge.

Each touch of Lady Bakshi-Mishra's hands sent sparks up Nat's limbs. Memories of touch, feeling, emotion. Memory of adrenaline. Want paired with the oh-so-desperately rare being wanted in return.

When they came together Lady Bakshi-Mishra leaned close to Nat to whisper, "You have more freckles than you used to."

Nat's eyes closed at the sensation of feather-light breath on their skin.

"I wonder if the spread as far down your neck as it looks like they do."

Nat let out a shaky breath. Thankful for the dance demanding the two separate, even if only for a moment.

It didn't last.

Lady Bakshi-Mishra's breath once again ghosted over Nat's ear. "Would you care to accompany me to the library?"

"You have a husband."

"He won't mind. We have an arrangement, and we're not exactly sharing those kinds of activities."

For pirates that arrangement would be called an open relationship, but that didn't exist outside of pirate society, at least not as far as Nat had seen.

As the pair split to continue the dance, Nat moving back toward Carrolline, they almost froze mid-dance step. It would have ground the whole quartet to a standstill. Rajni disappeared from their mind, her inappropriate offer long forgotten in the wake of that dark hair shining orange in the glow of the lights, far brighter than any Nat had seen its owner in before.

His dark eyes watched Nat like they were the only thing in the room. The only person worthy of any attention even as his mouth moved in conversation.

How could he be here? Was Nat just imagining it? Imagining him? But that would be absurd. For what reason would Nat be picturing *him* of all people *here* of all places?

The dance spun onward, blocking Nat's line of sight with frills and sparkles and excitable movement.

Their heart pounded in their ears, covering the sound of music. Leaving them with one singular thought. They needed to get to him.

18
What Are You Doing Here?

"Oh, Liege Adelhard, have you met Lord Liu?"

"Yes," Nat managed. "We're acquainted."

"He was just telling me about his travels." She kept speaking, her words lost like wind on the ocean. Nat only had eyes and ears for a single person.

They stepped close to him and hissed, "What are you doing here?"

Lord Liu smiled that impossible smile. "Is this not where everybody who is anybody would be?"

"We need to talk." They glanced around. "But not here."

Lord Liu turned to his previous conversational partner. "I do believe that young gentleman is attempting to gain your attention."

How was he so good at this already?

His previous conversational partner flushed, giggled, and disappeared across the ballroom.

With one last glance around, Nat muttered, "Come on." And began weaving between the guests.

They led Lord Liu into the only refuge likely to offer any privacy at an event like this. The place that had spelled disaster for Nat and got them banished to sea. The place all dandies and lieges tended to congregate. The library.

Shutting the door behind them both, Nat took a breath before turning to Tao. "What are you doing here?"

"I told you—"

"Not here: tonight at the ball. Here: Enderand. Here: Dinium. Here: high society."

"You're not the only one with a title." The same words Nat had once slurredly tossed at him, blood loss and fear and exhaustion wreaking havoc with their mental faculties.

"Somehow I don't think your title holds much weight here."

"You really think that after the way you behaved in my port, I wouldn't need to know what was going on?"

Nat folded their arms and leaned back against one of the book cases. Now that he mentioned it, they had been acting erratically ever since he found out their family name.

"I trade in information above all else." His graceful fingers traced the spines of the books next to Nat. Their eyes stayed glued to his hands as warmth coiled in their stomach.

Oh no. They should not have brought Tao in here.

Nat had spent too many interactions secreted away in libraries doing illicit things. The sounds of the ball carried in a muffled way under the silence stretching between them and Tao, the out of place Pirate Lord. A sound all too familiar to Nat, who had spent too many times covering that muffled music and conversation with harsh pants of their own and their temporary partner.

With Tao, Nat had been allowed to make noise. He had practically insisted upon it. As bossy during sex as he was the rest of the time.

And now, Nat couldn't help but picture the Pirate Lord, his slender fingers on Nat's skin, the way he flushed, the way his eyes had closed in exquisite pleasure. The rasp of his commanding voice.

"You're flushed," Tao said.

When had he looked at them? "It's warm in here," Nat lied.

Tao touched their bruised cheek with the back of his hand. "You don't look yourself."

"Foolish of me to not dress in purples to match it?" Yet another repeated phrase, this one, though, had been offered to Aleksei for bruises Nat had never been granted the opportunity to see, that first day on what was now *Mercy's Myth.*

Tao's dark eyes flashed that dangerous way they did.

Nat turned away roughly. Harsh against his softness. "Don't."

Tao huffed out a sigh. His breath ghosted over Nat's neck.

"I appreciate your concern, My Lord, but I would rather you refrain from such contact."

"Back to that, are we?"

"I don't know what you mean."

"After we fucked you started just talking."

Nat spun to face him again, anger swelling in their chest, bringing their shoulders up in a way that would have had Aleksei or Bear sighing that they'd never be a combatant. "Things aren't always simple enough to *just* talk. That's not what I do. Particularly here."

"Here in what exact capacity?"

"What?"

"Here: Enderand, Dinium, high society? Or here: in this book room with me?"

"Here: all of it." They pulled their hair off their face, only for it to bounce straight back into their vision. Little red coils springing like wind chimes. "This where I first—" They cut themself off. What was it about Tao that made them admit these things?

Tao's eyebrows rose. "You're thinking about that?"

"I always think about that with you." Nat slapped a hand over their mouth. They should *not* have said that.

Tao's attention fixed on them, oddly soft. "Always?"

Nat let their hand fall but said nothing. What could they say? They had promised Tao they weren't clingy. Tao had teased that he was more, better, more intense than their previous experience. And he had been right. At least in so far that being with Tao had been unlike anything Nat had experienced before.

But Nat had refuted the clinginess, and they stuck by that. To an extent. They had taken Tao's rejection in stride. Had accepted that it was a one-time deal. It just... wasn't so easy to forget and move on as Nat had hoped it would be.

"Dandy," Tao sighed. "If you wanted that, why didn't you ask?"

"Because you didn't want to."

"Such certainty."

"I'm not the only one able to ask."

"I could hardly have requested the sexual favours of a captain in my port."

Nat opened their mouth to argue, but no words came. Now that he put it like that...

Of course he hadn't said anything. Hadn't requested Nat's presence or attention that first time they had turned up all sparkling bronze as a newly minted captain.

And Nat had read rejection, so they had avoided, worked to get over it and move on.

"It doesn't matter," they muttered.

Tao caged them in against the bookshelves, a hand on each side of their head. They could duck out; escape the Pirate Lord's focus. But Nat was frozen. Heat swirled in their stomach. "It matters to me," he said in that deep, dark tone.

Nat shivered. "Why?"

"Because you're not the only one who thinks about that day."

19
Can't Risk Getting Caught

Nat's breath caught in their chest. Tao thought about them? About what they had shared? He, too, hadn't been able to move on?

"Dandy, you never leave my mind. You are a puzzle to solve and a dangerous one at that. I have known from the moment I saw you that I wouldn't be able to rest until I figured you out."

"So that's how long this can last? Until you think you have me figured out?"

"Does it matter?"

"What do you want?"

"A clue."

Nat surged to close to gap between them, hungry lips pressing insistently against Tao's.

He met their passion with his own. The hands that had caged Nat into the bookshelf grabbed at them. One sinking into their hair, the other wrapping around their waist, yanking their body against Tao's.

Long practised instinct led Nat's hands to the fastenings of Tao's trousers. It was simple work to undo them and slip their hand inside.

Tao made a strangled noise. His forehead crashed against Nat's shoulder, harsh panting filling Nat's ears.

The hand in Nat's hair tightened to the point of delicious, life affirming pain. They whimpered, tilting it back, exposing their throat.

"Fuck, Dandy," he huffed into their skin, nibbling with none of the precision he'd used the last time they did this. "You move fast."

Nat licked a stripe up Tao's neck. "You have to here. Can't risk getting caught." Their teeth nipped at his ear.

He shuddered, hand slipping from their waist to catch himself against the bookshelf behind them. The one in Nat's hair clung on for dear life.

Nat whined, tilted their chin, rolled their hips against the pirate apparently at their mercy. He took the hint, mouth pressing into their skin. Teeth and lips and tongue.

"This," Nat breathed, "is usually where we start trading information."

Tao groaned against their neck, making them buck under him, making them tighten their hand on him, making him writhe in turn.

"Like what you're really doing here."

"Following you."

"For what purpose? What do you want from me?"

"I want you."

Nat squirmed.

Tao's hand shifted from the bookshelf to Nat's trousers. He fumbled before managing to slip a hand inside.

Nat nibbled at his ear again, loosing a breathy laugh, tugging him even closer with a foot caught around his leg. "For what, exactly?"

"Because I like to play with dangerous things."

*N*at slipped out of Tao's caging hands as he panted for air, limbs trembling in the wake of their recent actions.

"You might want to clean yourself up and return to the great hall before anyone notices you're missing," they whispered to the Pirate Lord from the library door. "It wouldn't do to have a scandal."

Those were almost the exact words spoken to Nat that first time they had done this. The first time a fellow dandy had invited them away from the main body of the event.

"If you are caught," Nat added. "Please don't tell them it was me."

Tao turned his head toward them, but Nat slipped out of the door before he could say anything.

On the other side of the door, Nat pulled a handkerchief from their pocket and wiped at their hands. They brushed over their outfiture, ensuring everything was in its proper place, including their hair, and slipped back into the ballroom without fanfare, trying to forget the way Tao had chanted their name under his breath as he came undone in their hands.

Being with the Pirate Lord in his own port, in his own house, in his own bed had given him every possible piece of control. He had made the choices and Nat had been thrilled to be along for the ride. Here, Nat knew more, could do more, knew exactly what lines to walk. And the power was so new they didn't know what to do with the feeling.

20
Lie

$\mathcal{N}$at knew it was going to be bad when Lord Adelhard called them into his office once again after breakfast. This time he sat behind his desk, a barrier between himself and his child with their still bruised cheek. Nat couldn't say they were ungrateful for the barrier. Their face throbbed even now. But it felt far too reminiscent of when he had first banished them to sea.

"Where did you disappear to last night?" he asked.

"I'm sure I don't know what you mean," Nat lied.

"Your absence was notable. Particularly egregious when you had just danced with the woman with whom—"

"I was dancing with Carrolline. And Lady Bakshi-Mishra is married now."

"I will reiterate: I expect you to act in a way that enhances the Adelhard name, not a way that destroys it. Hold yourself to a higher standard. This is a tightly run ship."

"This is a household, not a ship. You aren't Admiral here, Sir." Their voice dripped with venom, pain dripping from their teeth and lips and tongue.

"Dismissed," Lord Adelhard ground out.

Nat pressed their tongue against their teeth, pressing the words against the sharp edges.

Dismissed? As if they were some naval lackey who was struggling to follow orders. Some poor conscripted young thing who hadn't had enough experience or training. It would have stung even if it had been the kind of 'dismissed' afforded to successful recruits, the kind of 'dismissed' Nat had only heard directed at others. But it wasn't. It was the same 'dismissed' that Rear-Admiral Eads had shot at them over and over again.

After Rear-Admiral Eads's unfavourable assessment of Nat in that first meeting, he had called his favoured crewman, Commander Rodgerson, to settle Nat onto the ship. Or 'Adelhard' as everyone on-board called them.

Dismissed.

When Nat hadn't settled in well, people had started to complain, they were called into Rear-Admiral Eads's office once again, told to buck up. That they had a proud naval family tradition to live up to.

Dismissed.

When Nat hadn't learnt their way around ship duties quickly enough — regardless of their lack of training — they were called into Rear-Admiral Eads's office once again, he set them to swabbing the decks as a punishment.

Dismissed.

When weeks of swabbing had left Nat's hands blistered and rubbed raw, they had gathered the courage to request an audience with the Rear-Admiral. They had asked him how long this punishment was intended to last. He had snapped that it would last until he told them it was over.

Dismissed.

Nat's fingers rubbed over the callouses those months of deck swabbing had left. Once blistered and bleeding and now scarred forever more. They turned away from Retired Admiral Adelhard and left his office.

Dismissed.

They left his door slightly ajar.

"*My* Liege?" Brett poked his head around the library door. "A Lord Liu to call on you."

"Liu? Here? Now?"

"Yes, My Liege." Brett's lips pressed together, the same expression he'd pulled when sixteen year-old Nat had tried to call the carriage for the first time on their own. "Am I correct in assuming no card was sent? Should I turn him away?"

"I'll see him. Thank you, Brett."

"Very well, My Liege."

Nat scrambled to their feet, cushions on the windowsill catching hold of one foot and setting them hopping as one tumbled to the floor. Tao didn't seem to notice, entering the room at Brett's invitation. The ageing butler showed himself out, off to fetch tea supplies, no doubt.

Tao stalked forward, teeth clenched together.

Nat's pulse picked up. This wasn't a playful kind of dangerous. This looked like serious, scary pirate kind of dangerous.

They backed away, stopping only as their back hit the wall.

"You just left me in that fucking library," Tao hissed.

Nat raised their hands in a gesture of surrender. "I couldn't stay. If I got caught there it would—"

Tao's hands slapped against the wall on either side of Nat, caging them in just as he had the previous night. "I am not some high society floozy to be... treated like that. Taken and tossed aside."

"Are you kidding me? When I bring up the prospect of mutual—" They glanced over Tao's shoulder at the door "—enjoyment, you get to give me a whole talk about how pi—people like you enjoy things and let them go but if I try to keep some kind of modicum of propriety about me, that's a problem for you?"

"Where was the propriety when you shoved your hand down my trousers?"

Nat's face heated, accompanied by a swirling warmth in their stomach. They smiled their dandified smile. "You telling me you didn't enjoy yourself, Princess?" they teased.

"You called me there talk."

"I got what I wanted."

"How?"

"You were very forthcoming."

Tao's eyes flashed that dark dangerous way once again. "I knew you were hiding something from me—"

"No shit!" Nat interrupted. "I've been hiding everything since day one. It's not a choice thing. It's survival."

"And when I found out your family name it all started to slot into place. You're just like *him*."

Nat's hand flashed out, shoving at Tao's shoulders. "Get away from me."

He didn't budge.

Nat shoved harder but it was no use. Tao was the Pirate Lord, had been a pirate and worked on ships for longer than Nat knew. Nat had less than two years experience doing anything but living a high society life. They weren't strong or experienced enough to move someone who didn't want to be moved.

"What I can't understand is how you had me and everyone else so fooled," Tao murmured.

"What is that supposed to mean?"

"*Mercy's Myth* is still in port, waiting for their voted-in captain to return. How long are you going to leave them to languish? Or is your plan to launch a naval campaign after them and take them all in? Earn your place in your father's footsteps?"

"I wouldn't do that."

"Such certainty."

"You can think what you want, My Lord, I don't care." Lie. "But that ship is filled with people who put their trust in me. I won't betray that."

"You already have."

And with that Tao was gone.

Nat sank down the wall, sitting on the floor of the library with tears welling in their eyes. Was he right? Had Nat already betrayed the trust of the entire ship?

"Tea, my Liege." Brett announced as he re-entered the library.

Nat wiped at their face, a futile attempt to look less disastrously crushed. The butler paused in the doorway.

"Shall I take it you won't be needing the second cup?"

"No, Brett. Thank you." Their voice came out shaky. The barely held back tears spilled down their cheeks.

China rattled as Brett placed the tea tray down. "May I ask what happened?"

Nat wiped at their face. "Disagreement."

"Must have been serious to leave you in this state. I remember the last time I saw you cry. It was when Carrolline broke her arm falling out of that tree."

Carrolline had always been an adventurous one, always wanted to follow Nat and do everything they did. Nat had tried their best to be a good elder sibling, tried their best to protect her when she needed protecting, and give her the confidence she needed to do what she could. She had insisted she was big enough to try climbing the tree on one of their many abscondments into the Adelhard grounds. Each avoiding a different type of lesson.

Nat had been convinced they'd be able to catch her if something went wrong. Convinced themself that Carrolline was right, she was big and strong enough to climb alone. Carrolline had slipped. Nat had leapt to try and catch her, to try and prevent her from hitting the ground. And they had failed.

That sickening snap of bone was one Nat would never forget. It had fuelled their nightmares for a long time.

And there she had been, sniffling on the ground and wanting her mama more than anyone else. Nat not enough to comfort her. They had run for the house, tried to get their father to help, but he had told them he couldn't understand them like that, that they needed to calm down. Nat had yelled that he needed to listen better.

That had been the first time their father had slapped them, sending them crashing to the ground.

Running from that room, they'd crashed into Brett, summoned by the commotion. Tears and snot streaming down their face, Nat had begged him to come with them.

Brett had set the injury, had comforted the young woman until she smiled again, had promised her a biscuit if she made it back to the house on her own two feet.

Nat had tried hiding in their room but Brett had come to clean up their ignored injuries too. The scrapes on their hands, and knees, and their cheek under where their father had slapped them.

"Your mother always said the answer to any problem lies beneath the weight of expectation and fear," Brett said. "I'm sure you'll find it."

He offered Nat his handkerchief and left them alone in the library.

21

I Don't Know If
I Can Go Back

The Adelhard breakfast table sat blissfully quiet. Lady Adelhard methodically buttered a slice of toast, steadfastly keeping her eyes on her own plate. Lord Adelhard ate slowly, gaze fixed on the dining room doors. Carrolline had laid her hands on the paper that morning, reading quietly as she ate.

Nat stared down into their tea, content to allow the calm to remain, even if it warned of a storm brewing. That same tension that had preceded the mutiny on what was now *Mercy's Myth* lay heavy over the table.

When plates had begun to empty and Lord Adelhard started to shift in his chair, Carrolline cleared her throat. "According to the papers, a naval vessel has just succeeded in an unintended rescue mission. Apparently The Royal Gladiator was found floating at sea, totally gutted."

"Hm," Lord Adelhard acknowledged.

The Royal Gladiator? Why did that sound familiar?

Carrolline continued, "According to this, most of the crew were left alive— even their commanding officer, one Commodore Ewart. How bizarre is that? Gutting a ship but leaving almost everyone on it alive!"

"Carrolline," Lady Adelhard hushed her.

"What?" Carrolline whined "It is bizarre. I thought pirates were meant to be ruthless. Why would ruthless vagabonds leave people alive?"

"So they can die slowly," Lord Adelhard's voice was quiet but it silenced the room once again.

Nat gulped. Gutted and left for dead? They needed to get down to *Mercy's Myth*.

Brett shuffled into the room, card clutched in his gloved fingers. He handed the card over to Lady Adelhard. The clink of her tea cup landing on her saucer, loud as canons, made Nat flinch. "In better news, your fiancé should be calling this afternoon."

"Is that a card from him?" Carrolline tried to disguise her grimace.

"Yes, with an apology for the delay."

"May I see?"

"No, you need to get ready."

"I have—" Nat started.

"To be ready to receive your sister's fiancé this afternoon?" Lady Adelhard finished. "Yes you do."

Outside the window the trees fluttered in the wind. It would have whipped Nat's hair about their face and filled the sails of *Mercy's Myth*. Perfect sailing weather. Perfect running away weather. But Nat wasn't on *Mercy's Myth*, or even outside in the wind. The layer of glass between Nat and the outside world reflected a shadow of their face back at them. Nat looked away from the distortion and toward the clock over the mantle.

Carrolline's fingers tapped against the arm of the sofa opposite Nat, loud in the otherwise silent room. It set Nat's teeth on edge.

"When is he supposed to arrive?" Lady Adelhard asked, not for the first time. She sat at a right angle to her daughter, facing toward the fireplace.

Lord Adelhard said nothing, his mouth pressed into a firm line.

The lingering echoes of their argument rang in Nat's ears.

"She is my daughter!" The shout had rung through Nat's bedroom wall as they changed. Shrill and reedy, in the way it only was when Lady Adelhard didn't care about being overheard.

Nat froze. They hadn't heard that tone of voice since before they were sent away.

"Do not raise your voice at me, wife!" Lord Adelhard roared in return.

Lady Adelhard did not heed her husband's demand. "You can hardly expect me to take this all in stride when I have yet to even meet the man to whom my only daughter will be bonded for the rest of her life!"

"He is the man I have chosen for her."

"You expect my trust of your judgement to override his insolence?"

"Insolence?"

"For a start he has yet to present himself, even at the engagement ball. And, as if that weren't enough, husband, he has yet to offer any kind of apology or explanation for any of this behaviour!"

So the apology had been a lie. That must have been why Lady Adelhard wouldn't let Carrolline see it.

"I'm sure he will provide an explanation in due course."

The thunk of a door slamming echoed down the corridor, Lady Adelhard's shoes clicking after it.

"I'm sure it's just the traffic," Carrolline offered into the tension filled parlour.

"The traffic?" Nat blurted.

Lord Adelhard's glare swung to Nat.

They pressed their lips together; resolving to keep their mouth shut, and listen to the clock tick and Carrolline tap until they were dismissed. Their leg seemed to disagree, bouncing in place where they sat on the windowsill.

Movement beyond the window drew Nat's attention. "Either the man of the hour is arriving or someone else wants to call on us," they hummed.

The carriage pulling into the Adelhard driveway was plain but for a small, simple crest painted on the door, the same colours as the driver's uniform. Nat didn't recognise it— what level of class was this family with such an austere carriage? How low had Lord Adelhard stooped to marry Carrolline off to someone with this as their carriage?

"Come away from that window, you look like a common nosy neighbour!"

Nat glanced at Lady Adelhard's frantically waving hands.

"We have an image to maintain. And while we're at it, choose a real seat; we can't have you loitering on a windowsill," she hissed.

By the time Nat turned back to the window, the cab was disappearing down the driveway once again, its passenger nowhere to be found.

Nat surged to their feet, legs itching to run. The quickest way out of the room would be through the windows, but that was little extreme for the current situation.

Brett shuffled into the room. "Captain Rodgerson."

Lord Adelhard smiled, a smile unlike any Nat had ever seen before, wide and genuine, almost proud. His deep blue jacket and waistcoat reminded Nat once again of a naval uniform.

Nat's heart seized in their chest at the appearance of the visitor. The thunder of rain on wooden decks filled their ears even as the bright August sunlight seeped into the room, warming their skin.

Rodgerson parted his hair on the left side of his head, lines from the comb trailed through the bland brown strands in a way that only occurred with liberal use of styling creams. His shirt was scruffier than Nat might have considered appropriate for a social visit with non-family.

Rodgerson almost hesitated at the sight of Nat. If they hadn't been so focused on him they wouldn't have even noticed.

"Charles!" Lord Adelhard clasped Rodgerson's hand, shaking it with rather more vigour than Nat might have expected. "Allow me to introduce you properly to my family, most importantly my daughter, Carrolline Adelhard."

Carrolline stood to curtsy.

Rodgerson offered her a stiff bow. He sat himself on the small sofa; the one designed to foster intimacy, but took up too much room to be able to share it. "I must offer my apologies," he began. "Got caught up on a rescue mission. Pirates. They besieged a fellow navy-man's ship. But I shan't distress the ladies with further talk of the fiends."

"The one who got his ship gutted?" Carrolline blurted.

Rodgerson jerked back, eyes narrowing. "How might a Lady such as yourself have learnt that?"

"It was in the paper."

"Carrolline, dear," Lady Adelhard interrupted. "Why not go see where Brett is with regard to the tea?"

"I'm sure he's just fine, my dear," Lord Adelhard challenged, setting a hand on top of his wife's. "After all, we must give out daughter a chance to meet her fiancé and vice versa."

Lady Adelhard pressed her lips together.

"I'll go," Nat volunteered quietly, slipping from the parlour and pressing the door closed with a finality that they wished would stick.

Fuck.

Their breath rasped up and down their throat, too much like the pain of nearly drowning. Was Nat drowning? How could they be drowning on land? In their childhood home?

How could Rodgerson be here? Nat hadn't seen him since— no! They wouldn't think of that.

"My Liege?" Brett's soft voice eased Nat out of the wordless spiral they had tumbled into.

"Brett," Nat stood up straight, trying to mask the way their breath still ricocheted around their chest. "I was sent for tea."

Brett looked down at the tea tray in his hands.

"Right," Nat sighed. "Of course you already have it. You're the perfect butler."

Brett raised one eyebrow.

Nat forced a neutral smile. "Apologies, Brett. I'm just struggling to think of Carrolline being married." It wasn't exactly a lie.

"I'm sure you aren't alone in that."

Nat glanced at the parlour door. "I don't know if I can go back in yet."

"My Liege?"

They ran their hands over their hair, pulling it away from their face. "I... I served with Rodgerson. He was on the ship... *The Valiant.*"

Fear. Rain. Shouting. Pain.

"He... wasn't very nice," Nat's voice barely escaped them.

22
He Thought I Was Dead... He Should Have Known Better

The Adelhard ballroom had been done up in blues this time. The naval uniform colour that Nat couldn't help but think would be a little tiring to see if one was actively an officer visiting the ball. But it wasn't Nat's decision. What Nat really hated, if they were being honest, was that the blueness of the curtains and tablecloths made it that much harder to avoid the actual uniformed officers that dotted the ballroom.

Rodgerson would be back, would turn up at this ball at some point. Every glimpse of neatly combed brown hair had Nat retreating on the off chance of running into him.

Upon returning from their tea retrieval mission, Nat hadn't been able to take in anything that passed in conversation. They had sat with the thunder of endless rain pounding against their ears even as the summer day outside continued it's clear and beautiful form.

After he had excused himself, Nat had remained in their seat, staring unseeingly into the silent and still fireplace. Sheeting rain in their eyes. Lady Adelhard had bustled Carrolline out of the room to prepare for the evening's events.

Lord Adelhard had stood, but hesitated before he began to move. "He looked at you like he'd seen a ghost."

Nat's head had jerked up. They knew their face still held that unfocused, haunted look but they couldn't seem to make it settle into neutrality or even a smile. Too focused on trying not to relive the worst day of their life. "I guess he thought I was dead."

Lord Adelhard's bushy eyebrows had drawn together. "We all did."

"But he should have known better."

With so little time and processing power left after the tea with Rodgerson, Nat had dressed in probably the most piratical of the outfits they had brought from the ship: a black waistcoat with green rope patterns all over it —one they had designed specifically for Tao's enjoyment before that awful captaincy presentation. The one they had apparently both read wrong. The shirt beneath was also black, a rarity in high society, the cravat matching the darkest green of the rope pattern. The jacket and trousers were both the palest green of that same rope pattern. All tied together with colour except for the decorative ropes around the cuffs of the jacket and trousers, a thin black strip with shining emerald accents.

"He's not here," Carrolline whispered, emerging from the crowd. Her ball gown was mostly white, decorated with sparkling blue and gold accents. Perfect pairing for a naval officer's uniform.

"What?" Nat turned away from their endlessly scanning the room, a dark head of hair pulling at their attention by the way it shone in the light. But there was no reason to look for that dark-haired person here. Tao would be long gone by now. He'd puzzled Nat out, realised they could never stop being an Adelhard. He would probably take *Mercy's Myth* with him. Unless he had another ship.

"Captain Rodgerson," Carrolline clarified. "He's not here."

"That man cannot keep time." The dandy-sigh at the end of the phrase saved Nat from sounding too much the pirate captain.

"And nobody will dance with me since I'm truly engaged now."

"How utterly ridiculous — plenty of engaged and married people dance."

"If he were here!" Carrolline cast her eye about the ballroom, searching once again. When she still didn't find the long awaited fiancé she turned up to Nat, expectant.

"What do you want me to do about it? Supernaturally summon him here?"

"Invite me to dance."

"But I just did that the other day," Nat whined quietly.

"Please?"

"You know I don't like to dance."

"But—"

"And even if I did, your first dance being with your sibling, it's not a great look."

"Nat—"

"And, maybe things have changed in the time I've been away and it's more inappropriate to dance with an engaged woman —certainly a dandy dancing with an engaged woman outside the presence of her fiancé."

"But—"

"But! Okay. Lady Adelhard, would you honour me with this dance?" Nat led Carrolline onto the dance floor.

Carrolline beamed as she followed Nat's uncertain lead. "You're so bad at this."

"Did you expect me to improve in the mere days since we last did this?"

Carrolline giggled, holding herself surprisingly well for a lady being kicked in the shins every few steps. Paired dancing was the worst! Yet, somehow, dancing with Carrolline calmed the beast roiling under Nat's skin, desperate for some semblance of safety even if it was falsified.

When the music finished, Carrolline led Nat to a cluster of blue coated gentlemen. Nat wanted to fight, wanted to dip away into the crowd. But they were helpless in Carrolline's hold.

"Lady Adelhard," Rodgerson greeted.

"Captain Rodgerson," Carrolline smiled shyly.

"Might I introduce my friend, Commodore Ewart."

The phantom flash of a sword swung in Nat's peripheral vision. The neatly pressed naval uniform made Nat's heart lurch in their chest. This uniform was either new or one left on land, unfaded by the sun, unstiffened by the sea air. His stripes glinted in the sunset streaming through the window behind Nat. The gold washed out his hair, making it appear dull and flat in its ponytail. How had a man so long in a seafaring career not gained the volume of everlasting salt like Nat had? His career must have been longer than Nat's, what with being a Commodore of a naval ship. At his neck, his cravat sat in a simple slip knot.

Oh no.

This was definitely the same Commodore Nat had fought with. The Commodore they had taken the cravat off and tied his hands with.

Nat needed to leave.

"Nat?" Carrolline called as they slipped out of her hold and shifted through the ballroom, a river around rocks, smooth and steady. Even as adrenaline spiked and their legs begged them to run, to push aside the people in their way, to leave as quickly as humanly possible. To flee, because the navy was in their spill.

23
Take Your Hands Off My Sister

Lord Adelhard caught Nat's arm before they could exit the ballroom. "Where do you think you're going?"

Nat's heart was battering against their rib cage like it wasn't going to wait for the rest of Nat to keep up with it. "I need to leave."

"You will do no such thing."

"Is everything okay over here?"

Nat flinched away from the voice, arm wrenching from Lord Adelhard's grip.

Carrolline's hand rested on Rodgerson's arm.

Nat's stomach roiled. "Take your hands off my sister," they snarled. "You utter piece of shit."

Carrolline stared at them, mouth open.

"There's no need for such language," Lord Adelhard admonished.

"If you don't take your fucking hands off her, call off the engagement, and never come near her again, I will tell everyone here and everywhere else I go for the rest of time *exactly* what you did to me."

"What he... did? Charles?"

Carrolline retreated from him, slipping into the crowd of guests.

"I did what I had to do," Rodgerson insisted.

Nat scoffed. "The eight months of bullying beforehand were necessary also?"

"Charles?" Lord Adelhard's voice turned deep and reproachful.

"We really don't need to talk about this here," Rodgerson pleaded.

"I think we need to talk about it," Lord Adelhard insisted.

"Rear-Admiral Eads had died. Murdered by pirates. I had to do what was necessary to protect the crew." The words came out rote. Practised. As if he had said it a hundred times before.

"What was necessary?" Nat spat.

"I had to put the crew first!" Rodgers advanced.

"I *was* crew!" The shout exploded from Nat without any thought, heedless of the ball fluttering around them all.

"Charles?" Lord Adelhard asked.

"Sure," Nat huffed out. "Ask him. Trust him. I'm leaving."

Lord Adelhard's hand wrapped around Nat's arm again.

"Perhaps we should go somewhere private to discuss this," Rodgerson hissed.

Lord Adelhard looked between his child, face still twisted and so far from its normal peaceful and dandified smile, and his almost son-in-law, pale as a man who had had his first run in with a ghost. "My study," he ordered. "Now."

$\mathcal{I}$n his office, Lord Adelhard's blue and white outfit called to his history in the navy, buttons sparkling in gold. He barred exit, for once being the one to stand by the door, the latch still visible, door slightly ajar and letting the light from the office spill out into the dark corridor. Nobody was supposed to be back here during the ball.

Rodgerson stood in the slightly worn down spot where Nat and apparently all Lord Adelhard's other guests tended to stand.

Nat shifted to the other side of the desk, by the big window. Could they climb out if necessary? How far would they get before one of the naval officers stepped in?

"I think you both owe me an explanation," Lord Adelhard demanded.

Rodgerson swallowed thickly, throat bobbing with the motion.

The music and conversation of the ball filtered through the wall, filling the silence when neither Nat nor Rodgerson spoke.

"I did what I had to do," he said again. "So few of us returned from *The Valliant's* mission. I kept the crew alive as best I could after the unfortunate demise of Rear-Admiral Eads."

"Kept the crew alive as best you could?" Lord Adelhard echoed.

Rodgerson's face paled but he stood rigid — plenty of naval training at standing to attention preventing him from sinking in on himself. At least he had the decency to show some shame on his face. "I did what I had to do."

"What you had to do?"

"For the life of the crew."

"But not my child?"

Rodgerson's under-bite stood out starkly with the tension in his jaw.

Lord Adelhard folded his arms. He turned his attention to Nat, pinning them to the spot.

Nat's breath shook in their lungs. They didn't want to remember. Not really. Didn't want to tell the story in front of their father. Didn't want to tell it at all. They had spent their entire time on a pirate ship trying to forget the events of that horrible night. But, like all truths contained too long, like their family name so well hidden for so long, it emerged.

"They set on us at night."

24
Damaged Merchandise

The yelling had wrenched Nat from sleep, the Rear-Admiral's booming voice calling everyone to man their positions. The other crew in the cabin scrambled to their feet, yanking on waistcoats and jackets and boots. And, more surprising, more terrifyingly, sword belts.

The man who slept below Nat, the one with the nasal whistle that kept Nat up all night, yanked Nat down by a leg. Their knee slamming against the ground with a thunk that carried over both the shouting and the raging storm outside.

"Get dressed," he demanded. "And man your fucking post!" Nobody said navy boys had any manners.

Their uniform had still been wet from the day working in the rainstorm, but they pulled it on anyway and emerged onto the main deck.

Nobody had supplied Nat with a sword.

Cold dripped down Nat's neck. In seconds the sheeting rain pinned their hair to their face. They flipped it out of their eyes as best they could, squinting through the deluge.

The crew of *The Valiant* clashed, locked in some kind of fight with... strangers in unfortunate choices of outfit. No uniforms, not a foreign navy then.

Swords clanged over the thundering of rain and boots on the deck. Nat cast about for a weapon, not that it would do them any good. Nat had never held a sword in their life. They'd never even been in a fight before.

A hulking brute of a man in an unbuttoned waistcoat appeared in front of Nat. The water dripping from his nose and blade only served to make him that much more intimidating. Nat's breath puffed in short bursts.

Was Nat going to faint? Actually faint? That would be new. At least if they fainted it wouldn't hurt when the giant man stabbed them.

Instead of stabbing them, his hand wrapped solidly over Nat's shoulder. He dragged a stumbling Nat into the centre of the deck where a host of the ship's crew had been corralled, penned in by the strangers. Blue jackets and white waistcoats puddled together like soapy water.

As the strangers rounded up and subdued the last few crew members, the sun began to peek over the horizon. The pink of the dawn seemed like an omen, a warning of blood to come.

With the uniforms, it was easy for the aggressors to single out Rear-Admiral Eads, his shining epaulettes glittering in the early light of dawn.

A pirate —they must be pirates after all— with a purple neck scarf circled the Rear-Admiral. Her sword remained level, aimed carefully at him as if the brute holding a dagger to his throat wouldn't keep him still. "How much do you care about your crew, Rear-Admiral?" She asked, voice husky but higher than Nat expected. "Could you pick a favourite?"

Nat couldn't help but glance at Commander Rodgerson. The bully. The man who had taken it upon himself to report Nat for every blunder, every mistake. The man who had decided Nat wasn't up to navy standards. The man who had gone out of his way over and over to ensure Nat remained below navy standards. He was the clear favourite. Everybody knew it. It was how he got away with that excuse for a cravat knot.

A huge bruiser of a pirate grabbed hold of Commander Rodgerson. How many hulking brutes did these pirates have? Compared to scrawny and under-nourished naval grunts...

"Would you choose one to take a punishment for the rest?" she purred.

Nat's attention snapped back to the pirate with the purple scarf. She must be the captain, surely.

"You want to punish my crew?" Rear-Admiral Eads asked. He stood straight, secure, seemingly unfazed by the dagger held to his throat.

"Here's the deal," she said as if the Rear-Admiral had said nothing. "You pick one of your crew to take the brunt of the punishment and — if they manage it with decorum, as you society types are so fond of — I'll let the rest of you go."

"And if they don't?"

"Then we keep trying until you're out of crew."

"I choose me. I will take the punishment."

Blood spurted from Rear-Admiral Eads's neck. His clean white shirt turned red, it seeped into his white waistcoat, his jacket collar and lapels. The pirate captain shoved his lifeless body toward the edge of the ship where it rolled into the sea.

She wiped her blade with the edge of her scarf.

Nat's stomach rolled, they clasped a hand to their mouth, looking desperately from pirate to pirate. There had to be some kind of escape. Nat was *not* dying out here in the middle of the ocean. And they were *most certainly not* doing it in this outfit!

One pirate in a baggy, poorly buttoned shirt turned his face away from the blood on the deck. His jaw stood out stark with tension. Disgusted? Maybe he would take pity on one little grunt like Nat. Maybe there was something Nat could offer him. Maybe.

Movement yanked Nat out of their planning. Commander Rodgerson now stood with the pirate captain. She asked him to pick someone.

Commander Rodgerson looked over the group. He lingered here and there. Finally his deep brown eyes landed on Nat.

No.

"That one." He pointed.

When the giant pirate who had dragged them onto the deck wrapped his hand over Nat's shoulder this time they couldn't feel it. The navy group seemed to part to allow them passage. Had they moved of their own accord or did the big burly guy push them? Nat didn't want the answer. They knew the answer. Nobody wanted the young dandy liege on the ship.

Nat's heart pounded against their ribs. Their stomach churned. Were they going to be sick? How undignified. Why were they concerned about dignity right now? Surely that was absurd.

"One slash for each crew member you wish to save." Captain Scarf pulled a dagger from her boot. She flipped it over in her hand and offered the handle to Commander Rodgerson. "Remember." She yanked it away when he reached to take it. "If you try anything other than your orders, you've doomed the whole crew."

Commander Rodgerson nodded sharply. He took the blade by the handle. Nat backed away, trying to remember how to breathe. Something was crushing their ribs, stopping them from pulling in oxygen.

"You sure we want to damage that one? Looks rich," someone asked.

"Who says you can't return damaged merchandise?"

Someone yanked the jacket from Nat's shoulders. They yelped, mindlessly reaching for the discarded item. Exposed. Vulnerable.

Rodgerson cut the sleeve of their shirt. Left arm. How ironic. That would be a mercy on anyone else, but Rodgerson knew better. Rodgerson knew Nat was left handed.

"Remember," the Pirate Captain's voice was sultry, "it only counts if they take it with composure."

Commander Rodgerson clamped a hand around Nat's wrist. The contact burned hot on Nat's chilled skin.

The slash across Nat's upper arm where their bicep met their deltoid didn't hurt as much as they had been expecting. Maybe it was the adrenaline? Maybe it was the cold? Maybe it was that their brain was so focused on remembering how to breathe?

The second slash brought pain with it. Nat tried to wrench their arm away.

Commander Rodgerson held too tightly. "Stay with it," he demanded.

Composure. That's what the Pirate Captain had said.

Three slashes. Did Nat want to save these people? Four. This crew that had done nothing pleasant for Nat at all? Another slash. Nat's head grew lighter. Another slash. These people, this crew didn't deserve to be saved.

Seven. But it wasn't about them. This choice didn't reflect on them. It reflected on Nat. Even if this was how Nat died...

Nat started to shiver. It was cold in the rain. Eight.

Fainting was a dandy's speciality. The only people more likely to faint than dandies were sheltered young girls on their first outings. Nine. Or pregnant people—they were very prone to fainting. Ten.

A muted "ow" escaped Nat. They almost laughed at the absurdity.

Eleven. Nat often chose to faint —well, fake a faint— when the situation called for it. Twelve. A simple one. No great flapping. No hand to the forehead.

The next slash produced a flinch, that one was deeper than the rest.

Nat was sensible enough to aim for a comfortable landing spot. Once it had even been a young lord who had taken Nat's fancy. Slash. They would count thirty heartbeats or so before 'waking' —unless smelling salts were called for. Nat could not abide smelling salts.

Slash. Fourteen? Fifteen? Nat had lost count.

They had never found the need to actually faint. Maybe it was because they had been young when their mother had died. Harder to shock?

Slash. Sticky, warm blood trailed down Nat's arm to where Commander Rodgerson held it, staining his hand. Another slash. How many people had they potentially kept alive? How many were left? Slash.

Fireflies had started dancing in Nat's vision.

Slash. Everything was too hot. Slash. Someone had submerged Nat's brain in a jar of liquid and was now shaking the jar. Slash. Their eyes fluttered, trying to close and stay open at the same time. Slash.

It was too bright behind closed eyelids. Slash.

25
Mercy Is You All Over

ears had spilled down Nat's cheeks, as they told the story. Quietly. Oh so quietly they whispered, "Next thing I know, I'm waking up in the brig of a pirate ship."

Lord Adelhard's jaw sat slack, his mouth open. Horror coated his face.

"I did what I had to do," Rodgerson whispered.

"No," Nat snarled. "I did what I had to do on that pirate ship. I kept my name to myself and I made the best of things. I used the skills I have to make myself useful. I stitched shirts and sails until my hands were bloody. I listened to the crew when they had nobody else to complain to. I charmed them with my dandy-ish ways that always seem to offend people like you."

"Mr Awthorn..." Lord Adelhard whispered.

"Mr Awthorn and Viscount Archin both gave up their family names to be ransomed back," Nat said. "Felitabby and I had no such recourse. He..." A shout in the pounding heat and humidity that warned of a storm. The flash of a blade. A body falling to the deck, blood pooling out around it. "Died. I wasn't so foolish as to believe you would pay."

Lord Adelhard stumbled back at the weight of the words.

"How... how did you escape?" Rodgerson's voice came out barely above a whisper.

"Like I said. I charmed them, made them trust me, and betrayed them."

"I don't understand. I was sure you would die."

Nat glared at him. "If you were so sure I would die, why would you choose me to take a slash for every member of *The Valliant's* crew? How could you look at the pathetic dandy, as you so often called me, and think I was the best person for the job?"

He said nothing.

"But you didn't, did you? You chose me for a purpose other than the one you were given. You risked the lives of an entire ship's worth of people for your pettiness. And for what? Because I like shiny clothes and talking fancy? Because I'm an Adelhard? Why?"

"Because everything was always handed to you!" Rodgerson yelled. "I had to fight my way up the chain of command, do shit you can't even dream of to get where I am."

"I have been imprisoned on a pirate ship," Nat interrupted. "Are you sure I couldn't dream of these things?"

"Everybody in the navy knows the Adelhard name. The prowess of the Adelhard family. And you turned up on *The Valiant* unable to even tie a simple knot. You offer nothing to the name and the legacy but you lucked into being the Adelhard heir! It's not fair."

"Life isn't fair," Nat spat. "It's our jobs as people to try and make it more fair not to hurt other people because of things outside of their control."

"That's not what the Adelhard legacy is about."

"I don't *care* about the Adelhard legacy!"

"You don't care about anything."

"Don't you *fucking* dare," Nat advanced on him. "I care about people. I care about my sister. I care about my crew. I care—"

"Your crew?" Lord Adelhard asked.

Whoops. Shouldn't have said that. "You think pirates would keep me in a cell not being ransomed for over a year?"

"You could have come home sooner?"

Nat looked over at their father. The man who had banished them to sea with a stone face. Who had seemed to hate every second of their being back. "Would you have wanted me to?"

The silence hung heavy.

Nat shook their head. "I'm leaving."

Lord Adelhard didn't move, still blocking the door.

Propriety and their hastily packed bag of clothes be damned, Nat had built an entire wardrobe at sea before, they could do it again. They just had to hope *Mercy's Myth* was still in port. That their crew hadn't got tired of waiting. Hadn't assumed Nat's extended absence meant they didn't intend to come back.

Even so, Nat could probably barter their way onto another ship, could get to one of the Pirate Ports, even without *Mercy's Myth.*

They climbed onto Lord Adelhard's desk chair, pushed the window open, and hopped out into the grounds.

Even if they wanted to stay, they couldn't. Commodore Ewart's very existence prevented that. Even if he hadn't made the connection between Liege Adelhard and the dandy pirate captain who had left him languishing at sea, he would eventually. Who knew relative mercy could bite so hard?

"You're leaving?" Carrolline whispered.

Nat spun to find her hiding in a patch of shadows by the window they'd just opened. Tear tracks lined her face, to match her sibling. She'd heard everything. Nat wished they could offer some comfort in the face of that but they had nothing left.

"I can't stay here," they whispered back. Would either Rodgerson or Lord Adelhard follow them out of the window? Or would they head for the front door first? Nat needed to move, to leave before either of them had a chance to truly process Nat's absence.

"Why not? Is it Captain Rodgerson? Father?"

"They don't help but it's... It's something else."

"The thing you've been hiding?"

Another glance at the window. No apparent followers. "One of them."

They started for the driveway. No way they'd get the Adelhard carriage out past the guests, even if that wouldn't have risked the driver reporting back where Nat had gone.

"Will I ever see you again?" Carrolline asked, follow Nat even at their clipped pace.

"I don't know. I got into some... difficult situations and I made choices that were appropriate to them that don't translate nearly so well to high society."

"Like Rodgerson doing what he had to?"

"No. I own up to these choices. I made them and I, mostly, stand by them. Some of them were bad, but they were all mine. I've never hurt anyone on purpose, Carrolline. For me, that's the line Rodgerson has crossed and doesn't want to accept. Refusing to admit you hurt someone doesn't make them any less hurt." They sighed, turning to face their sister. They owed her this much. "I know I'm hurting you by leaving again. And I really, truly am sorry for that. But my regret, my not wanting to hurt you, it isn't enough. It can't change my choices. Because one way or another, the situation has unfolded in such a way that I can choose to leave and probably live, or I choose to stay and..." They trailed off.

"Staying would kill you? That's a little melodramatic, Nat."

"I'm a pirate."

Carrolline's mouth dropped open.

"I'm *the* pirate that gutted that navy ship and left them for dead. Or, more accurately—" They rubbed their face "—to be rescued."

"I don't understand."

"It just seems fairer that way—"

"Not the mercy part, that's you all over. How are you a..." she dropped her voice to a whisper, "Pirate?"

"Short version, the navy ship our father sent me to was besieged by them and I... charmed my way out of the brig and into captaincy."

"You had sex with a pirate!?"

"No. Well, yes but not the way you're thinking. I actually charmed. With my words."

"But you have had sex with a pirate?"

"Yes, but again, that was a separate thing. He isn't on the ship; he runs one of the ports."

"There are Pirate Ports?"

"I really wasn't meant to tell you that."

The rattle of the Adelhard front door.

Nat surged forward to press a kiss to Carrolline's forehead. "Be strong, Cottontail. You're the sister of the one and only dandy pirate captain."

"Where are you?" Lord Adelhard bellowed into the dark night air.

Nat bolted down the driveway, stones crunching under their feet.

26
Now

Running was a foolish idea.

They should have snuck. Crept their way out after the ball had ended, disappeared out of the kitchen door and traipsed down the gravel coated driveway in the absolute dark of night. Or at least in a more sensible outfit than sage green.

Nat couldn't hope to be faster than a carriage. The road to Dinium proper and its docks, the road away from Adelhard Manor was a straight one. They had already been caught along it once. And, by the thunder of hooves behind them, they were about to be caught once again.

"Dandy."

That wasn't right. It should be a roar of 'stop' or 'you' or in the rarest of possibilities 'Nat'. But that... That sounded like Tao.

Nat turned. And there was the Pirate Lord. Illogically, impossibly halfway out of a carriage with his arm extended.

Nat caught his hand, letting him yank them into the box.

"What are you doing here?"

"You need to stop asking me that."

"Tao!"

He smiled. "I don't think I've ever heard you say my name before."

"I'm running away from my family home and the naval officers in it. Why are you here?"

The carriage jostled, tossing Tao into Nat. "I told you," he huffed, attempting to right himself. "You are a puzzle I need to solve."

"I thought you'd figured it out."

"So did I."

"Then what? You just had to be sure? Couldn't pass up the opportunity to risk yourself by coming into the home of your enemy once again? What?"

"Your people wouldn't listen to me."

"You tried to steal my ship!"

"Most Coded pirates have a greater level of respect for the Pirate Lords."

"Most Pirate Lords don't try to steal people's ships."

"I assumed you were never coming back."

"Why?"

"Because you are the heir of Admiral Adelhard."

Nat hesitated. "Did you tell them?"

"No."

"Why not?"

"Loyalty like you've inspired is impressive. When I became the Pirate Lord I had to use fear and conniving and blackmail to make it happen. You... Your crew loves you like nothing I've seen. You must have done something to inspire that. And the way you make me..."

"You?"

"Dandy," he sighed. "I have not been able to stop thinking about you since that first day I saw you in the tavern. And then we met and you were... The way you looked at me."

Nat had been running then too. Away from the ship that had imprisoned them, from the captain who had ordered their arm shredded. They'd dipped down a side street, pausing at the temptation offered by bao buns. Tao had offered them one, used the time to assess them. Nat had been so thrilled, after so many months at sea they had finally run across another dandy.

It had been a new kind of dandy game but slipping back into games at all had been so easy. So comfortable. So enticing. Made all the more so by Tao himself.

In the carriage, Tao ran soft fingers down Nat's cheek, tracing the lingering bruise there. "When Grigg found you, when I scared him off, I wanted to keep you forever."

"But that's not how things work," Nat breathed. They knew only too well, even after a single year of captaincy. "We can't be selfish when there are people under our care."

Carrolline. *Mercy's Myth.* Their fellow prisoners. Even the Adelhard family. Nat had always had to put their needs second at best.

Tao's face darkened. "And after I handed you back. What she did to you. The damage I had to—"

The carriage jerked to a stop, sending Tao out of his seat once again.

Nat peered out of the window. They'd arrived in town. Close to but not on top of the docks. They surged back into motion, leaping from the carriage and overpaying the driver.

Mercy's Myth had never looked so beautiful. The brown and white striped ship stood tall and proud over Nat even in the dimness of the night, lit primarily by its own on-board lanterns. Someone skittered across the rigging.

"Kajal?"

The boarding plank descended. Nat surged up it, presuming the Pirate Lord would follow. For the first time in their life, they had no concern about the swirling water beneath. Nat wasn't about to fall off the boarding plank now.

"*He* tried to make us leave without you," Kajal accused, pointing a finger at the Pirate Lord. "He claimed you weren't coming back. Tried to threaten us with becoming Un-Coded."

"But you're still here," Nat argued.

"I told you," Tao murmured. "Loyalty."

Nat waved a dismissive hand. "He got some bad intel. Are we all here?"

"For once."

"Then we make ready to leave."

"At first light?"

"At first chance."

Kajal frowned.

Nat took a breath, glancing over their shoulder at the docks, mind swimming with naval uniforms that didn't really exist, ears ringing with the thunder of carriage wheels. "If I promise to tell you all everything when we're on the way?"

"Prepare to sail!" Kajal cried, voice carrying from years of calling down from the rigging.

"Now?" someone else called back.

"Now," Nat bellowed.

27
Admiral Adelhard

"You're going to have to uphold your end of that bargain sooner or later," Tao murmured. He'd come to stand with Nat at the stern of the ship, as they scanned the horizon for the fluttering of white sails, for any hint that they were being followed.

There was a chance Lord Adelhard hadn't figured out their plan to head back to sea. But it was a small one.

"I know," Nat said.

"It's not going to get easier by procrastination."

They took enough time to shoot him a flat look. "I know."

"Spyglass?"

Nat took the gold cylinder from his offering hand, using it to search. Expecting to find the Enderand flag fluttering in the favouring winds, all strong stripes in bold colours, standing proud above a full contingent of shining white sails.

But there was nothing.

Haltingly, Nat returned the spyglass to the Pirate Lord. What had they been expecting, really? It would be far easier for Lord Adelhard if Nat did just disappear into the sunrise. He wouldn't even have to call off the wedding between Rodgerson and Carrolline if he didn't want to. Only the three of them officially knew what had taken place on *The Valiant* that night. Maybe Carrolline would leverage it; she had overheard everything after all. Nat could only hope.

But knowing in theory that their father wouldn't pay a ransom demand, no matter the threat against Nat, would always be different to being proven right. He wasn't coming. He wasn't sending anyone. He didn't want to rescue Nat. He never had. They pressed their hands against their face, leaning elbows on the stern of the ship. Always too much. Never enough. And now they had to admit everything to the crew with no hope of ever being able to return to their family, even if they had wanted to.

It wasn't like they *wanted* to end up in a huge, dramatic naval fight. It wasn't like they *wanted* to go back to being Liege Adelhard full time. They'd made the decision, probably would have even without Commodore Ewart's sudden appearance.

It still stung.

And now they had to come out to the crew. Had to risk it all knowing without a shadow of a doubt that all their most pessimistic thoughts about their father had turned out to be true. Fearing that their most pessimistic thoughts about the crew of *Mercy's Myth* might match up. What if they didn't want Nat when they knew? Nat had no life to go back to, nowhere to flee to. The idea of having to start all over again somewhere new with nothing, not even their family name to own...

They took a deep breath. Now or never. They stepped up in front of the wheel, slightly to one side so Hui could still see them. "There is something I have been hiding from you all," they announced. "Some of you know what it's about. Others of you probably don't. But it's why I asked you to dock in Dinium, why I've been gone. Where I've been gone."

Kajal paused their scramblings, hanging with their full attention on Nat. Even Aleksei had stopped working, like he didn't already know, having insisted on accompanying Nat to Carrolline's engagement ball.

Even in this awkward stillness, the ship held a beauty unlike anything Nat could make comparisons to. It was all the beauty of a dance and the freedom of that feeling of sitting above the sails. Every millimetre of the deck was filled with memories. Some good, like sharing banter with Aleksei and Jay in their sewing corner, like gifting Bear their cravat and seeing his soft smile, like climbing the rigging with Kajal and being gently teased for their lack of skills —always followed up by a comment about how long it took to learn these things. Some less good, like the main mast they had been tied to for sirens, the same one Aleksei had kissed them against on his captain's orders. Like the bow of the ship where Nat had been punished and had staged the mutiny against the previous captain. But even that torturous memory was mixed with playing mock trial and the crew using it as a stage for their plays.

This was their home.

They didn't want to leave it.

"Most of you were here when I first... boarded. But for those who don't know, I was a prisoner for ransom by the previous captain. Problem was she didn't know my family name. And that is something I still haven't shared with any of you." They took a deep breath and started to pace, unable to stand still in the face of the tension. "I want you to understand that it isn't a matter of trust—isn't *only* a matter of trust. It isn't necessarily that I assumed you would attempt to ransom me back as soon as you found out my family name. It isn't just that I knew I would be unransomable, no matter the cost. It's also a matter of who my family is. Who my father is. Who he was. The things he has done."

They took a shaky breath, leaning against the railing barring the upper deck from the main deck. A few of their crew had gathered there, looking up at them as if they were on stage and performing for applause.

Tao's comment about Nat picking up overripe fruit thrown at poor performers for their armour flashed in their mind. They glanced at him, still at the stern of the ship. Their heart throbbed in their chest to find he was still looking out over their spill, keeping up the rapt attention Nat hadn't been able to let go of for the entire morning of sailing.

The sun beat down onto the deck with all the power one would expect of this time of year.

"My name is Liege Nat Adelhard. My father is— was— is Admiral Adelhard."

28
Unransomable, Unwanted

Stars shone down at Nat, calm and everlasting in the midnight blue sky. They leaned over the edge of the ship. They should go to bed, the night crew could handle anything that needed handling, and Nat had been awake all the previous night and the entire day. But something prevented them from entering the captain's cabin on *Mercy's Myth*.

Grief at what had been lost. Carrolline. Their family home and all the memories contained within. Memories of their mother. Rajni. Jothi, even if xe hated Nat now. The life they had before. The idea of themself as Liege Nat Adelhard. Gone, forever out of reach.

The pain of the harshest truth Nat had always known and never wanted to risk proving true. Their father would not pay their ransom. He did not want them back. He would rather lose them to pirates and claim a good naval son-in-law to replace them with.

Fear that their crew wouldn't want them.

The revelation that Nat was the child of Admiral Adelhard had been taken surprisingly well, surprisingly easily. But Nat wasn't foolish enough to believe there would be no fallout. That none of their crew would have had run-ins with the Admiral who had branded Tao when he was only a child.

Only two of the crew had owned to it so far. Hui had gripped Nat's sleeve as they requested everyone return to duties, before they could think about moving away. "I had a run-in with him once," she whispered. "Admiral..." She trailed off, unwilling to say the name, as if it would summon him. That had never worked for Nat, wanted or otherwise. "On my parents' merchant ship. He didn't speak Shenai. He claimed we were pirates, even though we weren't." She looked at Nat with her impossibly dark eyes. "He killed my parents."

Nat had swallowed down the clog of tears welling in their throat. "Thank you for telling me. I understand..." They took a breath, a desperate attempt to steel themself. "I understand if you want to find another ship, or captain. If you can't divorce me from him and what he did. I know what it's like to lose a parent. If there's anything..."

Hui had said nothing more, her fingers unclenching from Nat's jacket.

Then, as the sun dipped over the horizon, Bear had caught them. "I knew your father," he signed.

Nat had rubbed their face. "How?"

"I served under him."

They almost believed they had misinterpreted the words. Almost couldn't believe that Bear, the scarred pirate, could ever have been navy. But it made the kind of sense that things you wished weren't true did. The uncomfortable kind.

"He was obsessed with ridding the sea of pirates. He would do anything if it meant he could take even one more out. That's how it happened." He touched a hand to the cravat at his neck, to the scar beneath it. "We were struggling to get by, beset by unfavourable winds and having been pulled off course by a kraken. But as soon as he saw a pirate ship he didn't care."

If Nat was being polite, they would call it single minded. More often they had termed him obsessive.

"We were in no shape to fight anyone, let alone recently resupplied pirates. I don't really remember what happened. All I know, all I remember was lying on the deck watching him. He saw me, recognised that I was alive, and chose to walk away."

Nat pressed a hand to their mouth.

"I woke up in the surgery on that ship. My own commander had left me behind to die and the pirates had patched me back together." He rubbed his neck again. "As best they could. I found out a few days later that it was Tao that did it." He glanced at the Pirate Lord, still at the stern of the ship, scanning the horizon. "He put me back together. But Baz... He kept me going."

"What happened?"

"I fucked it up. Didn't trust him with those pieces of myself. Thought I'd be too much. Got lost in the grief and anger and the desire for vengeance."

"Against the Adelhards?"

Bear's eyebrows knitted together. Tears filled his eyes and he nodded.

Nat closed their eyes. "You recognised me on *The Valiant.* That's why you picked me out for your captain."

The tears spilled down Bear's face, neat lines of liquid sparkling in the lamps swinging on the deck.

"Why didn't you just tell her my family name?"

"You're the first person to try and communicate with me since Baz. She wouldn't take information from me."

Nat swallowed thickly. "But Kajal and Jay..."

"Only started signing with me after you opened my world up with it. I owe you so much and I—"

Nat closed their hands around Bear's, preventing him from continuing. "Stop. I can't—I need time to process this."

Bear nodded.

Nat let his hands go.

"I'll understand if you want me to leave."

"No. Just..." They sighed. "No. This is your ship, I wouldn't do that."

Now alone, Nat dropped their head onto their hands. Their chest ached with the pain of it all. What would they do if the crew decided they didn't want Nat anymore? This ship was their whole world. They had chosen it above and beyond everything else. But that didn't mean the crew would feel the same.

And Nat couldn't resent them for it. Pirates voted in their captains. The crew should have the right.

A knock drew their attention over to the door of the captain's cabin. Dread filled them, another person come to claim links to Admiral Adelhard? They could ignore it; pretend they were asleep inside the cabin instead of hiding in a patch of shadow, watching from the deck. But no. That wouldn't be fair.

"Hello?" they called.

The figure turned to face Nat, moving over to them.

"I told them to make you up a bed," Nat offered the Pirate Lord. "They didn't put you in the cells or something did they? I really don't know what their problem with you is."

"No, they prepared me a bed."

"Oh. Good. Then why are you not in it?"

"You're not in bed either."

"You caught me." Nat leaned back on the rail. "Was there something you needed?"

"You."

Nat nodded. "What do you need me to do?"

Tao smiled that dangerous smile. "I don't think you really listened to me in that carriage."

"I *was* running for my life at the time."

"When are you not?"

Nat snorted a laugh. "I guess you bring it out in me."

"Nat." Serious.

Nat wracked their brain. They had been a little distracted at the time. They circled a hand, almost waving him off. "I asked what you were doing in a carriage near Adelhard Manor. You said something about puzzling me out, about the loyalty of my crew, about not being able to stop thinking about..."

"You."

Heat bloomed in Nat's cheeks. "Oh."

"I thought finding out your family name would solve the puzzle you presented, but it didn't. I thought following you here would do it, but it didn't. The way you were in the library was just more confusing pieces tossed over my table."

"Which library?"

"The one you fucked me in." He sighed, leaning against the railing next to Nat. "I don't think I've ever been hurt emotionally before. With Aleksei I was always waiting for the other shoe to drop, always aware that his loyalty was torn, always prepared for him to pick his captain's orders over his feelings."

"It's who he is," Nat mused, thinking about Lord Roydon's confession. Claiming you'd give up a lot for someone wasn't necessarily the same as actually doing it. Still, maybe Nat should offer him the option.

"And with others it was always the same. Brief interludes. Fun shared and ended. Never anything that could create emotional pain. I had thought that was what I shared with you."

"A brief tryst," Nat agreed. "That's what I thought too." It had matched their experience to such a great extent that it just confirmed the idea that Nat didn't have the capacity for that kind of love.

"I thought I only cared about puzzling you out because I hadn't solved it yet. But after you pulled me away from that ball and then just coldly left me there I was hurt. And I didn't know what to do with it. And then you were so unchanged by it."

"Unchanged by it?"

"You're very obviously a high society type, a liege. Talk of mutual pleasure should have scandalised you, but you laughed at me when I suggested Aleksei would have been your first. And, even when we..."

"Fucked?"

Tao's mouth twitched. "Yes. In my palace, you seemed so unfazed, as if this were all just a normal day for you. Thinking back on it after the library, nursing my hurt, I couldn't understand it. How could I have been left so shaken and you just adapted? I wanted to make you react."

"I'm a dandy."

"So you've said."

"Everybody thinks dandies are just foppish, fashionable types but," They unbuttoned their shirt cuff, pulling their sleeve up to reveal the tattoo nestled in the crook of their elbow. "We're this. We linger on the edges of society and make our homes there. We flirt with scandal, trade in information, and accept that nobody *wants* to marry a dandy, so we might as well find pleasure elsewhere. We're the cutting edge of fashion because we listen. We're foppish as a ruse. Even fainting is usually faked. The first time you met me, I had been on a navy ship for eight months living through hell, had been all-but tortured, and then spent I don't even know how long in the brig of a pirate ship. My whole world was nothing like what I had experience with. Honestly, you were the most comfortable thing in it. You're a dandy."

Tao tilted his head back to look at the stars, processing.

Nat followed his gaze, using the sparkling night sky to distance themself from the emotion of their next question. "Where do we go from here?"

"The ship or...?"

"I am still the heir to the man who branded you. I can't ever leave that fact behind. I won't ever not be that."

"You told me when we met that you were unransomable. When I found out who your father was, I thought it was because any pirate who had had a run in with him would have killed you for it." He looked at Nat, dark eyes sparkling in the low light from the swinging lanterns just out of reach. "Now, I think I understand what you meant."

For the first time since returning to the ship, Nat pulled their dandy persona around them. They smiled. Shrugged a shoulder. "Such is life I suppose. You get used to not being what people want."

"Oh, Dandy..."

They pushed away from the rail. "I should probably actually get some sleep." Starting toward the door to the captain's cabin, they spun to face Tao, walking backwards as any captain worth their title could. Knowing every millimetre of their ship. "You should too."

"Is that an invitation?"

29

Fool On Me

The sunlight washing through the windows that lined the rear of the captain's cabin on *Mercy's Myth* prodded Nat into wakefulness. Their head ached and they loosed a quiet groan, snuggling deeper into the covers. A mirroring groan sounded.

Nat jerked awake.

Tucked up next to them in the bed, the Pirate Lord slept. His breathing even and slow.

A soft smile stole over Nat's face. They trailed fingers over his form, not quite making contact. Circles of bruises dotted his bared torso. Proof of Nat's ministrations the previous night.

Tao had all but chased them into their cabin when Nat had spun away with the answer to his question its own question, "Why don't you come and find out?"

Nat had been ready, but had still squealed when he yanked them back toward him, hands immediately leaping to tug at their cravat.

"I have not been able to stop thinking about doing that to you," he said into Nat's newly exposed neck. Nat shivered as Tao's warm fingers pressed into the hollow of their throat. Intensely vulnerable and all the more excited for it.

They tipped their head back and whispered into his ear, "You going to take off your shirt this time, Princess?"

"You going to let me into your bed this time, Dandy?" he teased right back, teeth nipping at Nat's earlobe.

Nat had slipped out of his grasp, spinning to face him once again with a teasing grin stretching over their mouth, their fingers flying over the buttons of their waistcoat. "Not just into my bed."

"If what we did in the library is your usual experience does that mean...?"

"You are officially the only person to see me shirtless? Yes."

What Nat could only describe as the look of the Pirate Lord stole over Tao's face. A sort of possessiveness and greed that was everything Nat had always thought pirates would be. The part of them long contained, smushed down to the tiniest space because it didn't quite fit in the box Nat was supposed to form inside, had always wondered what it would feel like to be viewed that way. It sent a tingling thrill up Nat's spine.

He stalked toward them before they could get the waistcoat off their shoulders. Slipping hands inside, sliding along their soft shirt and tugging it out from where it was carefully tucked inside their trousers. "I guess we both have seen things of one another that we rarely share."

Foolish emotion welled in Nat's chest and leaked from their eyes. They swiped a hand over it, futilely hoping Tao wouldn't notice. But of course he did. He was a dandy.

"Nat?"

"Sorry. I'm being too much. Just didn't realise you trusted me so much."

Tao cupped their face. "Too much?"

Nat shook their head.

"I do trust you. Fool on me."

Nat was halfway convinced to see what results kissing Tao awake would achieve when the door opened, morning light spilling in from another angle.

"Captain," Aleksei knocked despite already being most of the way into the room. This crew and their inability to respect privacy. He froze, eyes flicking between Nat and the now awake Tao, visibly naked, in their bed. His mouth opened and closed, no words escaping.

"Yes?" Nat asked. At least they were turned away from the door so Aleksei could only see their shoulder. At least Tao's long hidden brand scar was easy enough to cover with the tiniest shift of Nat's hand.

"Are we heading to Shenai?" he spluttered.

"What do you think?" Nat asked Tao. "Want to be held on my ship for a little longer or head straight home?"

"I think we need to take a little time to ensure the navy is not following before we risk heading to my port."

Nat looked back over at Aleksei. "So, Shenai-wards but the long way around, okay?"

"Of course," he squeaked, retreating from the cabin.

Nat smushed their face into the pillow. "Fuck, that was embarrassing."

"You ashamed to be with the Pirate Lord?"

"I'm ashamed to be found naked in bed with him, yeah."

"Why didn't you lock the door?"

"It doesn't have a lock."

"Why doesn't your crew respect your privacy?"

"Your guess is as good as mine; I've been trying to convince them of the benefits of knocking for a year now."

Tao stretched, body shifting at Nat's side. "Do you think he'll tell?"

"It's Aleksei."

Tao shifted. "If your whole crew already knows then..." He kissed Nat's shoulder.

"You're incorrigible."

"You're irresistible."

"As much I might like to stay here with you all day, I do have a ship to manage."

"Can I ask you something?"

The tone shift almost threw Nat off. "You can ask."

"That story you told, in your father's study, is it true?"

Cold washed through Nat. They were too exposed for this. Too vulnerable. They swallowed. "Yes."

They clambered over Tao, slipping out of the bed with none of their usual elegance and dancing to pull something from their wardrobe, hiding behind the changing screen as Tao, still lounging in the bed, asked, "And that was on this ship?"

"Yes."

"And you stayed? Not only stayed but staged a mutiny against the pirate who did that to you?"

Nat stopped dressing, pausing where they stood. Their voice came out soft. "They asked me to."

It seemed the Pirate Lord was content to leave it there, saying nothing more. Nat continued dressing.

Emerging from behind the screen in yet another green outfit —really, it was definitely too abundant a colour in their wardrobe, especially having left so many other options at Adelhard Manor— Nat brushed a hand over their hair. It was too long, at this rate they would have to start tying it back. They headed for the door, freezing once again, their hand on the door handle as Tao asked, "How do you bear it?"

"If they wanted to hurt me, they would have done it already." They smiled. "Help yourself to my wardrobe if you like."

"Claiming the Pirate Lord through attire? Very sneaky."

Nat laughed as they emerged onto deck, closing the door behind them.

The wind whipped their too long hair around their face, fresh sea air filling their lungs. Their mother and Brett had been right. The answer to any problem lay beneath the weight of expectation and fear.

Nat had been expected to remain a liege, had been afraid to admit their origins to the ship. There was still a lot to do. The fallout of everything that had happened wasn't over yet. And Nat wasn't so foolish as to believe beginning a relationship with the Pirate Lord wouldn't come with its own challenges. There would be plenty to deal with.

But, for possibly the first time in their entire life, Nat felt free and, more importantly, happy.

Epilogue
To Claim A Pirate Lord

Shenai Pirate Port's inescapable humidity pressed against Nat, the most telling sign for the still-new pirate that they were close. Anticipation sparked under their skin at the thought of returning for the first time since dropping the Pirate Lord off in his home territory.

It had been almost half a year since then. The winter chill had settled in everywhere else and Nat's crew would be happy to spend time somewhere warmer, even if Shenai's warmth did come with that pressing humidity as part and parcel. They could have gone to the Dry Sea, but Nat had preferences and they were learning to balance those with the needs of the crew.

Nat grabbed hold of a safety line, wrapping it around their torso before beginning their unsteady climb up the rigging. Kajal, spider extraordinaire and official rigger of *Mercy's Myth*, laughed at Nat's inexperience and eagerness in equal measure.

"We'll make a rigger of you yet, captain," they teased.

Nat took enough time to stick their tongue out at Kajal. Once they reached the top, they settled themself on the sail's crossbar, holding tight with their hands as they peered at the horizon.

It would have been easier to take up a position on the bow of the ship with the spyglass Tao had left behind, but Nat liked to avoid that particular area whenever possible. It had been the regular haunt of the previous captain and the more distance Nat could keep from her and her legacy the better for everyone involved.

The port itself sat on a hill. Flat- and arch-roofed buildings clustered together, leading up to the pagoda-style, red-roofed palace of the Pirate Lord Himself.

The smile threatened to break Nat's face.

"Maybe thirty minutes, Captain," Aleksei called up from the deck. "You might want to come down soon."

"You all think I'm so bad at climbing," Nat huffed. "I've only fallen twice!"

At least since they'd been an official pirate. They'd also fallen when they were still a prisoner who traded their sewing skills for relative safety and freedom, which had resulted in having to climb up the rigging to fix a broken piece of sail. The first time subsequent to their election to captaincy had been on their way to meet the Pirate Lord of the Dry Sea. The second time had been right in front of Shenai's Pirate Lord, who had relentlessly teased Nat about getting tangled in the ropes up until Nat had tied him to their headboard with their own cravat and asked him whether he would like to be teased.

But Nat did start climbing down after one last look out over the vast endlessness of the ocean. They had been right that first time. It was impossible to get tired of a view like this.

When it came to Pirate Lords, they liked gifts and, after thorough discussion, it had been agreed that despite the nature of their relationship shifting, Nat would still be expected to bring tribute in return for the benefits offered by being in a Coded Pirate Port.

Tao traded in information, and, lucky for Nat, so did they. Which made coming up with tribute to offer Tao much easier than almost any of the other Pirate Lords. Especially since Aleksei was still writing those stories. They packed another leather-wrapped paper tribute away into a case, no point getting it sweaty on the walk up to the palace, and emerged from their cabin freshly dressed and more than ready.

"Captain," Jay called.

"Yes?" Nat asked.

"The crew says you're all hyped up about going to see the Pirate Lord but you'll come to the tavern with us first, won't you?"

"You just want me to buy a round," Nat teased.

"No, we just want to spend time with you. Come on, back to the place we decided to mutiny."

"When you say it like that it makes me nervous," Nat sing-songed but they let Jay and the others lead them to the tavern anyway.

It was just as bustling as Nat would have expected at this time of day, at this time of year. A song was already in full swing when the crew of *Mercy's Myth* entered in a huge group. Behind the bar Lin folded her arms, as if daring them to start moving her tables.

"You remember what we agreed," Nat called over the bustle and music. "No ruining Lin's nice establishment, okay? The tables stay where they are."

"Or at least we put them back after," Bear signed.

"Bear!"

He shrugged, the picture of innocence.

Someone grabbed Nat by the hand, flinging them into the midst of the song and dance. Someone else caught them and tugged them into a jarring leap of a waltz-like something. Spinning around and around. Nat traded from one partner to another, giddy and sweating until finally the song came to its close and they could excuse themself toward the bar.

"Typically," the smooth, even voice that had been fuelling Nat's fantasies for the last six months spoke closer to Nat's ear than he should have been able to get without them noticing. "A captain is supposed to present tribute to the Pirate Lord before frolicking in the tavern or any other such use of the port."

Nat spun to face the speaker, fighting a smile. "My most sincere apologies. But it seems the Pirate Lord is not in his palace right now to offer the tribute to."

Tao's eyes sparkled. "Perhaps he saw a ship of ruffians approaching and decided to come down to protect his people."

"Ruffians! I'll have you know my crew is the most impeccably dressed in all the known and unknown seas. Even the sirens sing so."

"Another run in with sirens?"

Nat waved a hand. "We have an accord."

"You have an accord with sirens?"

"Are you surprised?"

"Do you have my tribute?"

An evasion. Nat smiled. They looked down at their empty hands. "I did..." They scanned the tavern for their crew or their tribute case. Aleksei had taken up his favourite booth with a few of the others, including the newest member of Nat's crew: one ex-Lord Kingston Victor Roydon, Roy to the crew, Victor to his boyfriend –the whole reason he had decided to take up a life of piracy. Aleksei's arm sat around Roy's shoulders, a soft, private smile gracing both of their faces.

The tribute sat on the table top. Trust Aleksei to show some kind of sense.

"Ah."

Before they could head toward it, Tao's fingers laced with theirs. "Later."

"But it's right here and I won't—"

"Aleksei will bring it."

Nat let the Pirate Lord tug them out of the tavern, into the bright sunlight of Shenai, and all the way up the hill to his palace. They entered through the same side door Tao had first led them through, bypassing the throne room altogether, dipping down green and gold corridors. Nat expected to find themself in the room with the green velvet sofas, the one that led off to a secreted bedroom, the same one they had first been together with the Pirate Lord in. Instead, Tao led them into a different room.

They stopped just inside the door. This room was surprisingly modest. A simple bed, a wardrobe, and a changing screen not unlike the one in Nat's cabin aboard *Mercy's Myth*. "Is this... your real bedroom?"

"Of course."

The sun shone bright through the wide window, screened with fabric to allow some visibility outward but little the opposite way, if the gold pattern on the hemmed sections was anything to judge by. The windowsill itself was as red as the roof of the building but the walls were a pale white-green. Beneath Nat's feet soft rugs coated the wooden floor.

"You really do trust me."

Tao wrapped his arms around their waist, settling his chin on their shoulder. "Should I not?"

Nat turned to kiss his cheek. "Just thinking about how lucky I am."

"Do tell."

Nat laughed. "Shall I extoll your virtues, My Lord?"

"No Princess today?"

"We're only just getting started."

Tao's hands shifted to the hollow of Nat's throat, reaching for a cravat that wasn't there. "No cravat?"

"Sorry, didn't think of it."

His hands shifted to unbutton Nat's shirt. "I thought you liked them."

"I do sometimes."

Tao's hands slipped inside Nat's shirt, tracing lines over their chest. Nat squirmed in his arms. "I guess that means we won't be playing those kinds of games?"

"Presumptive, Princess."

Tao smiled against Nat's skin. "If you didn't care so much about your clothes, I'd have half a mind to tear them open, buttons be damned."

"Then I'm very glad you know I care so much about my clothes."

"Off with them."

"Bossy," Nat teased but did as he bade, fingers flying over their waistcoat and shirt buttons as only one with many years of practise could do.

They stood, shirtless, before Tao, his eyes raking over them, expression shifting at the line of scars down Nat's dominant left arm. He refocused too quickly for it to ruin the mood. "You appear to still be wearing trousers."

"Oh, am I the only one divesting myself of clothing?"

"If you would like my clothes removed, you need to show initiative, Captain."

Nat reached for the buttons over Tao's shoulder.

He stepped out of their reach. "But first, do as the Pirate Lord bids."

Getting out of their boots was always more complicated than Nat wanted it to be. But the boots had proven necessary on board the ship and Aleksei had promised that, with a simple tie under the knee, they would be far easier and more waterproof than the full-lace naval boots Nat had still been sporting. They should have known better than to trust Aleksei for fashion advice.

Nat capsized halfway onto the bed.

Tao snorted.

"They're new, okay," Nat grumbled.

Tao sank to one knee, deft fingers untying the back of the boots with surprising ease. Slipping them off Nat's legs even easier.

Nat ran a soft hand through his hair, freed from its usual plait. "You're unnaturally pretty, you know that."

Tao smiled up at them. "Not one I've heard before."

Nat cupped his face with that same hand. "It's true. You're the most beautiful person I've ever met."

"You're just saying that because I'm on my knees."

Nat leaned forward to press their lips against his. Tao's hands landed on their thighs, making them squirm again and wish they had succeeded in getting their trousers off already.

They slipped their hand down from his face to undo the buttons of his shirt only for Tao to pull back again. Nat grumbled a groan.

"Trousers, Dandy."

Nat flopped somewhat undignifiedly backwards onto the bed, lifting their hips only long enough to slide their trousers off before grabbing Tao by the back of his head and tugging him in for another kiss. They ran fingernails over his scalp, swallowing his moans.

They tugged the Pirate Lord up by his hair until he had them pressed back against the bed, fitting his hips against theirs. They squirmed, sliding hands under Tao's shirt, revelling in the feel of his skin.

They'd missed this. Half a year was too long. And, while Nat could have found relief, scratched an itch with anyone else from a random Pirate Port, it wouldn't be Tao.

"So many thoughts, Dandy," Tao murmured. "Do you care to share any of them?"

"Have you been with anyone else since...?"

"Jealous?"

"No. Yes? I'm not sure."

"We hadn't discussed it."

They hadn't. It had been difficult to find the time for many discussions of important, feelings-related subjects. Between Nat's return to their ship, the revelation of their family name, and both their and Tao's inability to be alone together without devolving into at least kisses, there hadn't been much time for such things. Particularly when those kisses were so often interrupted by Nat's crew's lack of boundaries.

It probably meant he had. Why wouldn't he? He was the Pirate Lord after all. He had plentiful others to warm his bed. Or whatever the phrase might be in Shenai, where it was unreasonably warm for most of the year. That was fine. Really, it was. Nat could hardly attempt to hold him to a request they hadn't even made.

"So I thought it best to not," he finished.

Nat shoved out from under him. "You what?"

"Why?" Tao rolled onto one side, cushioning his hand under his head. "Have you been sowing wild oats?"

"Is that really the euphemism you're going with?"

"Are you avoiding the question?"

"I haven't been with anyone else since the first time we were together."

"That explains why you're gagging for it."

"I am not gagging for it! Who came down to meet who at the docks in this equation?"

"I can't believe I brought you into my actual, personal bedroom and you're picking a fight."

Nat pressed their mouth closed. They couldn't believe he'd let them into his actual personal bedroom at all.

Tao had freely admitted he hadn't been able to get Nat out of his head since their first meeting. Why were they still so nervous about his affections? About his commitment?

"I missed you," they admitted. "It's not the same without you. The ship feels empty. My cabin is... It's never really felt like mine. But when you were in it with me, it was so much closer."

Tao trailed a hand down Nat's unscarred arm. "It's a challenge."

Nat smiled. "But I don't need to make it more challenging?"

"We'll figure it out. It took you a year to figure out being a pirate."

If they even had yet.

Nat sighed and flopped back down on the bed, covering their face with their hands. "This is not what I pictured when we set out toward Shenai."

Tao's fingers traced patterns over Nat's stomach, shockingly platonic considering they were naked and half-naked respectively. "What were you picturing?"

"Oh, you know, I'd come up to your princess tower and kiss you awake."

Tao nipped Nat's ribs.

They squealed.

"Have I been fuelling your fantasies, Dandy?"

"I bet you've been fuelling more than just *my* fantasies."

The hand on their stomach trailed down to their hips, platonic touches shifting, sending warmth spiralling in Nat's stomach. "Tell me about one of your fantasies."

Nat swallowed thickly, heart thumping against their sternum. Their face heated, inevitably turning as red as their hair. The concept of telling Tao the exact positions they'd pictured him in; the way imaging his tongue, or that look in his eye, or the way his face flushed had set Nat off. The fact that they had had to sneak away to their cabin in stolen moments with just their own hands for company and desperately hoping their invasive crew didn't barge in at exactly the wrong moment. The coiling heat in their stomach whenever they thought of Tao. The image of him coated in bruises from love bites and spread across the bed of their cabin. The fact that Nat still had shirts that smelled like him.

They shook their head. It was too much. Nat had been raised in high society, admitting to having fantasies was already outside their comfort zone. Even so, the concept fanned the flamed of their desire, making them squirm under Tao's gentle touches.

Tao's breath ghosted over their ear and down their neck. "Go on," he breathed, licking over the shell of Nat's ear. "Just one."

Nat's mouth opened with panting gasps. But no words came. They got lodged in Nat's throat. Nat gripped the bedsheets tightly in their hands, knuckles whitening. They were a pirate now, had actively chosen this life, actively left high society by their own reckoning, but it still held such a hold over them.

"Do you remember the first time we kissed?" they finally managed.

Tao smiled against their skin. "I remember later that day."

Nat let out a breathy laugh. "No. That first kiss, we started fighting then too."

"Argumentative, aren't you?"

"Me?"

"Go on," Tao encouraged, shifting to look up at Nat with that same intense attention he always did.

"You requested a kiss as a boon for taking care of my injuries. And I called you—"

"Peaches," he said the word with distaste.

"And you called me Dandy with that same tone." They swallowed. "Like it was both an accusation and not a bad thing."

Tao's eyes flitted from Nat's face to their chest, to the line of scars up their arm and the tattoo nestled in their elbow.

"The way you wield power," Nat prompted.

A smile crept over Tao's face. "You want me to exert my power over you? I am surprised, Dandy, the way you were talking earlier, I almost expected that you would want to claim the Pirate Lord."

Nat turned, tugging Tao in by the back of his neck. "I already did that on my ship. Isn't it only fair to give you a turn to do the claiming?"

Not The Ignorant Kind

Short Story

Tao's perspective of his first meeting with
Nat and the puzzle they present him with.

ao didn't like to not know things. Mysteries could be fun to unravel, but only because Tao was already so skilled at discovering things people wanted to keep hidden. Training as a physician had only increased Tao's desire to know all, see all, understand all. And it had given him tools by which to gather extra information. Knowledge about bodies that told all kinds of stories. A flush here, a stance there. Between that extra knowledge and Tao's way with words, most people decided to give in and tell him their secrets. He would find out one way or another anyway, why not mitigate the potential damage and scrutiny by telling on themselves? Which was probably why this particular puzzle has so thoroughly claimed his attention.

In one of the many offices he had in a building too big for one simple man to live, but that was of an appropriate size and stature for someone in his position, Tao had laid all his clues across a low table. He scoured the notes, the pieces of a life he had managed to gather, what little of it there was to find. Part of the problem was that he had so little to base his search on in the first place. It didn't matter the tools or the people at his disposal if the only certainties he had were low enough to count on one hand.

Worse still, almost all of it had come in one fell swoop. Further interactions with the source of the puzzle had yielded so little information that Tao almost felt he was swimming against a riptide. It would be easier to let it go. But Tao wasn't that kind of person.

His first puzzle piece had been an accent. But not just the accent, the choice of words too. It had been clear from the first sentence, *"I'm a tad low on funds."*

In the bright, relentless sunlight they had narrowed their eyes, eyebrows drawn low in an attempt to see past it. If they stayed out for much longer with that peach toned skin, they would burn in those squint lines. They looked different out here compared to when he had seen them in the tavern a few days earlier. Not just for the sheepish smile, but so many other things too. Their stance, their attitude. None of that happy confidence showed here and now in the marketplace. And wasn't that interesting.

The way they said those words, though. *Tad. Low on funds.* It all added up to a person of high society. This was a person not used to asking for favours. A person used to having enough money for the things they desired.

The way their mouth formed the words told Tao all too easily that Endrish was their first language. Which could have been more useful, had Enderand not conquered half the known world at this point. They could be from anywhere with an accent like that.

The name had been easy to find too. At least a first name. He'd admitted to not having seen them before. Met with the easy agreement of a simple, "No."

"*I'm Tao,*" he had offered.

"*Nat.*" Could be short for something. But the way they said it, the way they later responded to it didn't match that. Usually people with nicknames carried an air of apprehension. Constantly on edge, waiting for someone to expand said nickname into its fuller version. Nat didn't do that. They introduced their first name casually, more casually than they probably should have considering the situation they were in at the time. Still, Nat as a name wasn't particularly popular so it should have helped.

It hadn't.

Tao also had a ship name. Not just the one they had, as it turned out, been captured to. That one had been easily found, though reluctantly given as part of their introductions.

"*What ship are you with?*" he had asked after hearing their name, filing it away. It was the kind of question he would ask any newcomer to his port. Made all the more relevant and important by Nat's obviously ill-fitting clothes and interrupted stance. They held themself awkwardly, but Tao couldn't tell if they were hurt or simply on the run.

They hadn't responded. Worse still, they had frozen. A wide-eyed little fawn in the middle of wolf territory. All pirates could sense a weakness like that. And something about Nat, even then, said they should have known better than to do something so foolish as display their fear.

Tao had reassured, placated. After all, he always found these things out. He didn't need Nat to tell him. And the guard they had run from interrupting their conversation, face chilli red with rage only confirmed Tao's thoughts. He didn't need them to tell. He found out.

Not only was Nat with *Poseidon's* but they were a prisoner.

Poseidon's was a particular kind of ship. They liked to skirt the edge of the Pirate Code like it was a blade to walk upon.

Playing with boundaries was one thing. *Poseidon's* took it to an all new level. Which explained why Tao had involved himself quite so intricately. He'd snapped at the crewman about letting prisoners wander free about his port.

Nat had slumped at his side. Defeated. Depressed. And how interesting it had been, to watch the wind fall from their sails as if they hadn't been obviously blowing them with a straw. To see all the thousand possibilities flittering around them crumple to the ground like mosquitos in a sudden rain.

So Tao had involved himself further. He stole them. Temporarily. Wanting to see how much he could find out. What a fool he had been. He should have let them go then and there. Not started himself down this path.

But he had been sunk on this —on them— since that day Aleksei had brought them into the tavern. Seeing the way the red-haired stranger had transformed from shy, nervous even, into a part of the action of the tavern. The way they had lit up at being invited to dance, to share in the shanty with the other pirates. To believe Tao had felt any other way would be a lie.

For that temporary rescue he had been rewarded with yet more tidbits of information. Confirmation that Nat was a member of high society. Implication that their family was in some kind of trouble. The knowledge that they were unwanted. That they had been hurt. And not just by pirates. He still couldn't escape the image of that moment of weakness where every piece of carefully curated persona had faded away to reveal a young person convinced the world was made entirely of pain.

"Ultimately, if you want to hurt me you will. That's just how it works. People justify

it but there are lines they will cross and lines they won't. I have almost no control over it. If you want to hurt me, you will, my scrabbling to stay safe doesn't really change anything except where the lines lie."

The problem with Nat, and the puzzle they presented, was it, and they, were too confusing. And too intriguing for it. One moment they were the blushing liege, turning away to provide privacy to a mere caress of the face. The next, they asked frank questions like, *"Did you love him?"* as if it weren't a monumental sort of ask. As if to answer wouldn't be world shattering. Power imbalancing. As if such questions were easy.

After that, after reluctantly returning them to the person who wished to hold them for ransom, he had found the ship Nat had been on before their capture by pirates. *Poseidon's* quartermaster had been exceedingly forthcoming. He always was. Aleksei...

Nat had been captured from *The Valiant.* Naval ship for sure, even if he hadn't figured that out for himself already.

They couldn't have been aboard ships at all for more than a year. Their hair too soft, their enjoyment of food too fresh. They weren't resigned to a life at sea. So he'd used his contacts and influence to fish out the last few years of *The Valliant's* records.

Now, knelt on the mat at his squat dark wood table, he checked over them again, knowing there was nobody who could possibly have been Nat on the lists he had managed to find. Barely any N's at all. Nobody with a Nat in their name. Let alone record of someone whose official, legal name was Nat. But the last set of records were long gone, lost to that boarding that had brought Nat into his life.

When he wanted a positive spin, he considered it useful to back up his hypothesis that Nat hadn't been at sea long when they first met. When he felt defeated, it was more useless. It told him nothing about Nat at all.

Tao hated nothing so much as useless and unrelated pieces of information. Hated that it had to be him that was the problem. Not quick enough to put it together. A patient presenting with symptoms that didn't make sense and he not able to fix it. Attempts to find a root cause that resulted in more theorising and less discovery and the entire time the patient was worsening.

His intent focus on the puzzle of Nat was taking time away from his duties. He wasn't playing the game half as well as he had used to, but that first time Nat had turned up in his receiving room after being voted in as captain of what was now named *Mercy's Myth*. That first time he had seen them after their fight...

They had strode in with Aleksei at their side. A Deity and their worshipper all decked out in matching attire. Bronze thread glittered, complimenting their bright red hair, even if it clashed just a little with their pale, peachy skin.

Tao had found himself out of his chair without even realising he'd stood. He walked around them, taking in everything about the way they had chosen to present themself. The version of themself they wanted to show the world. It matched so neatly with what Tao had expected, so neatly with what Tao had offered them when he had made clothes to replace the aged and ill-fitting atrocities he'd first seen them in.

He'd almost been proud.

And then they'd snapped at him, "I am not a carousel to be circled over and over."

He'd fired back, "Then why are you dressed like one?"

He'd expected laughter. It hadn't come. Still too wrapped up in the self-deprecation and fear. Sourness fizzled in the air, lemon juice blasting out of the squeezed fruit.

While Nat had become more confident, more taunting, more... piratical than Tao could ever have imagined them to be, he didn't trust it.

That soft, weak, lonely dandy couldn't fool him with shiny clothes and sharp words. Tao was the Pirate Lord of Shenai. He had been voted in by his people to protect them. To hold the visitors at their port to the Pirate Code. He couldn't risk betraying that trust and, if Nat would not tell him their loyalties, their allegiance, their origins, then he would find out for himself.

But not today apparently. The papers strewn across his desk showed no new insight. No sudden inspiration struck him as he, once again, traced an approximation of that mysterious tattoo on their forearm.

The paper felt nothing like Nat's smooth, soft skin under his fingers. Nothing like the warmth of their body pressed close to his. Nothing like the trust they had shown him in such a brief instance. He had broken their trust back then. Too nosy. Too insistent.

Tao had never been one for simple pleasure to turn into something more serious. He was the Pirate Lord; he couldn't afford to split his loyalties like that. The closest he had ever come to serious had proven that to him more clearly than anything else could have. Aleksei had been torn between his loyalty to his captain and his affection for Tao. It had been easier for all involved for Tao to cut him loose. After all, better to have the hurt under his control, better to make the hurt happen when he was prepared to deal with it, rather than the hurt of a betrayal. Rather than finding out whose side Aleksei would ultimately fall on. Better to choose to let go of that care and affection than to find out you were the one who cared more.

But somehow Tao had fallen prey to that same problem in Nat. A new variant for sure, but the same basic problem. He seemed to care. More than he should. And he needed to know who they had been before he met them before that care could turn to anything else. He needed that barrier. He needed to keep himself and his people safe.

A knock called his attention to the door. "Enter," he commanded.

Xiran slipped through the door with smooth and graceful movement. In her hands she held a folded piece of paper. She spoke in Shenai. "I think I have something for you."

"You think?"

She nodded.

"Is it not addressed to me?"

"It is not."

"But you think it is for me anyway?"

She held out the paper, hovering by the door as if afraid of what Tao's reaction might be. As if reluctant to hand over the very thing she had entered the room to bring him.

Tao stood, hand outstretched. The paper was soft, clearly of high quality. Heavy in an awkward way, weighted unevenly. Tao's fingers brushed a wax seal, a family crest embellished upon the ruby deposit. The same colour as Nat's hair.

He flipped the paper over. The handwriting was flourishing. A dip pen in pure black ink with enough practise to leave no sign of smudging, even on the widest and most decorative loops. His stomach went cold at the words themselves, fingers clamping tight to the paper.

Xiran was right to have been afraid to bring this to him. Just as she had been right that he needed to see it. This was the key that unlocked the puzzle of Nat.

Their family wasn't in dire straits. The reason Nat couldn't have been ransomed back was this.

"Thank you, Xiran. That will be all for now."

She slipped from the room as smooth and quietly as she had entered, leaving him alone with the letter addressed oh so carefully.

Tao touched fingers to his collarbone, to the scar that the Admiral had branded him with when he was a youngster on his first ship. The thing that had pushed him into medicine in the first place. A scar that had never healed right. Never would. The piece of himself that would always carry that horrible run in with that Admiral with the voice of Davy Jones himself.

Apparently Nat's father.

And Tao could only assume that, as with any other high society family, Nat was loyal to their father above and beyond all else. Just as a true pirate was loyal to their captain. And just as Tao himself was loyal to his people.

Tao looked down again at the puzzle pieces spread out across his table. This puzzle, he supposed, had always been leading to one inevitable conclusion. He was always going to find out where Nat was from. Was always going to find out why they were hiding it. The only thing left to do was confirm it.

To confront them with this knowledge. But this wasn't just any person, wasn't as simple as watching for regular reactions. Nat was almost too well practised at hiding their thoughts, at speaking in innuendo and almost statements. It was what made those rare vulnerabilities so intriguing, so welcome, so desperately wanted.

No, this would require something more intricate. The initial accusation and then…

Tao knelt at the table again and started writing notes, creating a path for Nat to follow, a treasure map bringing them back to that room he had once bared himself to them in with so simple a question as *"Did you love him?"* And so simple an answer as *"Once."*

He would lead them there, and he would find out, once and for all, where their loyalties lay.

Not The Wanting Kind

Short Story

Tao's perspective of Chapters 18 Why Are You Here? & 19 Can't Risk Getting Caught.

Seeing Nat engage in the high society version of dancing was nothing akin to having seen them swept up in the shanty as the tavern in Shenai Pirate Port. There, Nat had been all smiles, and gracefully accepting a lead, and bright shining eyes. Here, Nat's mouth was set in something that looked like a smile but certainly wasn't. Their movements were stiff, dance partners not quite so skilled at hiding their expressions grimacing as Nat stumbled into them over and over again. It was almost unbearable to watch, but Tao couldn't tear his eyes away. Even as he exchanged pleasantries with a young woman endlessly glancing over her shoulder at a young man with his nose buried in a pretty glass of yellow-ish punch.

The moment Nat spotted Tao in return, their stance changed. Shoulders drawing up and back, suddenly the tall, proud, pirate captain even in the glittering visage of a high society dandy. Suddenly Nat, when before there had been some pale imitation.

That shift did something to Tao, something the curious, betrayed part of him didn't want to feel. Something akin to interest—not the unravelling interest, no that same interest that had pulled him to invite Nat into his bed in the first place.

The way they stalked over to him was as a predatory cat, gone was that weak fawn in the wolf den he had seen once, that first conversation in Shenai, and here instead was a *pirate*.

They exchanged words, Tao got rid of his previous conversational partner, followed Nat's order to accompany them out of the ballroom and found himself secluded with them in a room entirely walled in books. With the door closed, most of the chatter and music from the ball was hushed to almost silence. Nat leaned against one wall of books, bright sparks of hair and outfit and those piercing eyes shining with such a dull background. Their attention flicked to the door before focusing on Tao.

"What are you doing here?" they demanded again, closing themself off with arms folded over their chest. A barrier.

Something about the way they stood spoke of pain. Like an injury somewhere inside their torso or, no, the expectation of pain to come. Tao's attention fixed on the bruise coating half their face. It hugged their eye, shifting over their cheekbone and disrupting the pattern of their freckles with a swash of purple and speckled red.

Tao went to repeat his earlier answer to the same question in the ballroom, that everyone who was anyone would be in attendance of this particular event, but Nat cut him off, demanding the specifics of why, for the first time since he had become Pirate Lord of Shenai, he had left his port.

"You really think that, after the way you behaved in my port, I wouldn't need to know what was going on?" He trailed his fingers across the leather bound books, needing a reprieve from the intensity of Nat's assessment. Needing to breathe before anger became too violent in the face of what had obviously been done to them.

Tao would recognise the aftermath of a slap whenever he saw one. He was more than a little familiar with them, both as a recipient and as a ship's surgeon. He wanted to take Nat by the shoulders and shake them. To demand that they tell him who had hurt them so he could exact revenge. Needed to bundle them up in his arms and protect them from ever having to face such harshness again. And he could do none of that because he still didn't trust them. How could he after what their father had done to him all those years ago?

Admiral Adelhard's effect on the piratical world knew no bounds. He was the threat people only whispered of. So few of them survived run-ins with the man that it only enhanced his image. If any other pirate found out that Nat was his child—his *heir* they would have killed them where they stood and sent the body back to him in pieces.

No wonder Nat had claimed themself unransomable. And to think, Tao had believed, naïve and stupidly, that it was because they were just as alone as he was.

"I trade in information above all else," Tao said, more to the books than to Nat.

When the dandy didn't respond, Tao glanced at them once again. Their face was flushed as red as their hair, eyes distant but trained on Tao's fingers against the books.

"You're flushed," he observed.

They jerked, almost a flinch, eyes casting down as if ducking away, ceding command and control to Tao. Not even bothering to fight for it. Their knuckles whitened where they held the cuffs of their sleeves. It ached in Tao's chest to see someone so animated turn into this closed off version of themself. "It's warm in here."

Tao found himself brushing gentle knuckles over the bruise marring Nat's cheek. "You don't look yourself."

"Foolish of me not to dress in purples to match it?"

It should have been funny. Should have been spoken with levity, even if that levity was falsified. He wanted nothing so much as to bring back the Nat he had grown to—

"Don't." Nat cut off his thought process with a harsh word thrown out and followed by a blast of movement. They turned away from him, jerking his hand off their face in the process.

Tao sighed, letting his hands fall to his sides. There could be no clearer confirmation that, despite his feelings and despite the way it seemed like Nat responded to him, they truly did not want to repeat the experiences they had shared in Shenai before Nat truly became a pirate. He couldn't blame them. The way they had fought after the fact still burned in Tao's stomach too.

"I appreciate your concern, My Lord, but I would rather you refrain from such contact."

"Back to that, are we?" All hyper-formality and closed clipped words.

"I don't know what you mean."

"After we fucked you started just talking." Open and mostly honest. And then that fucking fight had ruined even that.

Nat spun to face him again, all anger prickling at their edges.

Tao stepped back.

Through bared teeth, Nat snapped. "Things aren't always simple enough to *just talk.* That's not what I do. Especially here."

It was all too easy to step up to the fight presented. Tao was, after all, a career pirate. "Here in what capacity?"

"What?"

"Here: Enderand, Dinium, high society?" He fired their earlier words back at them. "Or here: in this book room with me?"

"Here: all of it. This is where I first—" They cut themself off, face somehow flushing further, the redness of it creeping into their hairline and down what Tao could see of their neck, hidden by shirt collar and cravat.

"You're thinking about that?" About their first experience, which had apparently been sequestered away in a musty room full of books and with the very intense risk of being caught. No wonder Tao's receiving bedroom hadn't fazed them. No wonder they had laughed at him for his questions about their experience. No wonder they could move on so easily.

"I always think about that with you."

"Always?" Tao breathed.

Upon their return to his port, all trussed up and newly captained, when they had snapped that they were not a carousel to be circled? When they had presented the dirty stories Aleksei wrote as tribute? When they had come into his receiving room and he had admitted his meeting with their father?

All those times Tao had teetered on the edge of saying something and choosing instead to remain silent, Nat had been doing the same?

"Dandy, if you wanted that, why didn't you ask?"

"Because you didn't want to."

"Such certainty."

"I'm not the only one able to ask."

"I could hardly have requested the sexual favours of a captain in my port."

Nat opened and closed their mouth, pulling their lips into a thoughtful pout. They shook their head. "It doesn't matter."

Because they were planning to stay here? Because something else had changed? Tao pinned them against the books before they could walk away. "It matters to me."

A delicate shudder rippled over them. "Why?"

"Because you are not the only one who thinks about that day. Dandy, you never leave my mind. You are a puzzle to solve and a dangerous one at that. I have known from the moment I saw you that I wouldn't be able to rest until I figured you out."

Nat tilted their chin up at him, a challenge and the spark of an invitation all at once. "So that's how long it can last?" They challenged. "Until you think you have me figured out?"

Tao had never known someone so full of contradiction before. Someone who could somehow swap from elegant innocent liege to confident or even cocky pirate captain in the blink of an eye. But that was the appeal of Nat, wasn't it? That they could so rapidly shift into whatever form suited them most at the time? And that was he intrigue. And, of course, the irresistibility of struggling to keep up when Tao was usually three steps ahead of his conversational partners. And the addictiveness of seeing the hints of reality beneath. The realest and truest form of Nat that only appeared in infrequent glimpses.

Tao had seen it when Nat had fallen into their melancholic speech about how the world would hurt you, how Tao would hurt them if he wanted to, regardless of what Nat did. It had hit him so hard he'd ended up reaching for his secreted wine. He'd seen it again when they asked if he loved Aleksei. When they laughed at Tao for believing they might not have experienced intimacy before. And finally in those moments of intimacy shared, the aftercare with hands trailing across partly bared bodies. And again, in a brief blip, when Tao had revealed he knew their family name.

"Does it matter?" He asked in place of an answer. He hadn't lied when he said pirates found pleasure with one another for as long as it lasted and didn't ascribe shame for those things ending. But he couldn't confirm that he would ever figure Nat out to his satisfaction. Couldn't promise he would retain interest in them if he did.

"What do you want?" Nat asked, but it sounded like a flirt.

You, but that would be too obvious, too on the nose, it didn't fit the game Nat had laid out for Tao to play with. "A clue."

And they were kissing him, dragging him against their body and pressing their lips to his insistently.

It was like water to a parched man. Quenching something Tao didn't even know he wanted and yet stoking his need for even more of it. He found his hands grabbing at Nat, burying one in their hair and the other clutching tight to their waist. The warmth and weight of them pressed against him burned like the sun.

A strangled noise escaped Tao when Nat's hand slipped into his trousers. His legs trembled, knees threatening to give way beneath him as his whole body spasmed at Nat's ministrations. His whole world shrank to Nat. Nat's hands on him, their breath in his ear just as ragged as his own, the scent of them filling his nose.

They tilted their head back, exposing their throat and it took neither thought no effort for Tao to turn and press his mouth into that newly exposed skin. "Fuck, Dandy, you move fast."

Last time they had done this, it had been a long and luxuriating thing. The time before, an exploration of each other for the first time.

Nat's warm tongue painted up Tao's neck and his hips bucked into their hand. Completely overcome with want. Want he had been staving off for a year.

"You have to be here," Nat whispered, nipping at Tao's ear. "Can't risk getting caught."

The words fanned the flames even higher. Tao caught himself against the bookshelf at Nat's back as his knees buckled. Saving himself the indignity of sliding or crashing to the ground. He had never wanted something—someone so badly in his life. And the threat of being seen...

He returned to nipping and sucking at Nat's neck, torn between wanting to leave marks, stake his claim, and not wanting to add to the bruises already marring their fair skin.

"This is usually where we start trading information," Nat murmured, voice breathy but shockingly coherent.

How they could still formulate words, Tao couldn't begin to explain. How could they contemplate conversation at a time like this?

"Like what you're really doing here."

"Following you," Tao admitted into the warm sharp edge of their jaw.

"For what purpose? What do you want from me?"

Isn't it obvious? "I want you."

Against him, at his words, Nat squirmed.

Desperately uncoordinated hands tugged inefficiently at the dandy's clothes, coming up against the struggle of modern fashion.

Nat tugged him closer with a leg hooked around his, using the same shelf Tao had used to keep himself upright as a perch and squirming endlessly against him. Making his blood boil and his head spin with pleasure.

"For what exactly?" they asked, words separated by rough pants of pleasure at Tao's own affections.

Tao searched his pleasure-hazed brain for how to answer that question. How to respond to the predator whose jaws he was entirely enthusiastically trapped within. Nat's affections never stilled, preventing Tao from pulling together more than a few words at a time. "Because I like to play with dangerous things."

Nat's groan in Tao's ear turned his focus into a golden haze of pleasure. More words whispered in his ears spurred him on. He couldn't have begun to say what those words were, what he responded to them with. Nat toyed with him, spurring him onwards and further into the spiral of his own feeling until it exploded into an inferno.

Tao found himself panting into the wall of books, barely holding himself upright in the wake of their attentions. He trembled, world shifting back into focus and reality as Nat slipped out of his grip. The sound of the door at his back, the sudden rise in the volume of the party noises, told all too well that Nat was leaving.

"You might want to clean yourself up and return to the great hall before anyone notices you're missing. It wouldn't do to have a scandal."

Perhaps, in another state, Tao might have picked up on the lingering devastation contained in those words. Might have puzzled out the years of isolation and subtle rejections Nat was drawing upon to say them. But flushed and messy and breathless with sweat cooling down his spine and imminent solitude creating an ache in his bones, Tao had no space to think about such things.

"If you are caught," Nat continued. "Please don't tell them it was me."

Tao turned toward Nat. "Dandy, I—" But Nat was gone, the door shutting behind them with a quiet click, returning Tao to that almost silence.

His stomach twisted, acid burning up his throat. Letting his knees collapse him to the floor and caring not a jot for his state of undress, Tao questioned how it could be that every Adelhard he ran across caught him so thoroughly unprepared? How was it that both Adelhards managed to find his weakest points and both could leave him fighting down an unbearable bubbling in his chest and stomach? Aching in a way he had never hurt before?

How could Nat leave him here like this? Was this what all their previous experience before Tao or piracy had been like? No hope of the care that Tao had grown to expect? Was this how Nat had first been introduced to intimacy? Just the act of sex and none of the care?

Tao took a deep breath, steeling himself against the feeling, the sympathy for Nat. Sympathy could only take him so far anyway, and Nat Adelhard did not seem to need nor desire any of his feeling. Sympathy or otherwise.

He tidied his clothes and headed for the windows, large enough to fit through easily. So what if somebody noticed he was missing? Tao wasn't an actual part of this ridiculous society and he didn't need to play by their rules. Didn't need to play by Nat's rules.

Despite the agony of isolation, the way his stomach had shifted from a warm and delicious swirling to churning and acidic, Tao was still the Pirate Lord of Shenai and he wouldn't be toyed with like that.

Can't Wait For More From Will?
Join The Mailing List At:
WillSoulsbyMcCreath.com
For exclusive and early
access to more of their
stories.

About The Author

It's pronounced "Souls-Bee-Muh-Kreth"
As a cosplayer, Table-Top Gaming nerd, and videogamer; fiction has been a staple of Will's life forever. They like to corrupt their friends into joining these pass-times, or at least reading their stories.
Obsessed with every way to tell a story and every possible use for one, Will had few choices other than becoming a writer. A little too nosy for their own good they like to invest their time fixing other people's problems, and when that doesn't work they hand out stories to make you feel better.

Turn The Page For A Preview
From Will's Upcoming Urban
Fantasy Series

Claretbury Chronicles

Claretbury Chronicles

Contents Subject To Change

The white paper envelope of a bill or bank statement hung halfway out of Billie's letter box, caught in the metal plate. They would have left it, the Guild dealt with all Billie's necessities but the ash black wax seal drew their attention.

Tearing through the wax released the unmistakable smoke-scent of magic. It would have been panic-worthy had the seal not been decorated. A simple, interwoven H and G: The Hunters Guild.

Like every other letter from the Hunter's Guild, it was impersonally type-writered; letters smudged and uneven in a way that had, at first, been jarring. Was still jarring when it had been a while since last contact. What few letters Billie got, bank statements and invoices, were printed computer text — letters spaced even and neat in perfectly measured rows. No misaligned keys. But the Guild used type-writers because they were more resistant to magic.

Billie scanned the page and flung it onto the shitty dining table that filled far too much of their studio flat — Guild procured, of course.

Moving. Again.

At least this time they hadn't thrown out the boxes for their stuff. Not that they'd be able to take much of it with them. Not as far as they were headed. So much for Billie maintaining a specific area of the country.

Billie had been an active member of the Hunter's Guild since their teenage years, when their natural arkte powers had manifest amongst the other horrors of puberty. Go figure, most magic manifested either in toddler years or in puberty. Ironically, being an arkte was the least traumatising part for Billie. At least until the Guild had come to collect them. Then it had been 'off to boarding school' also known as stuck in elite monster hunting training with the rest of the arktoi.

Unfortunately for Billie, the Guild was used to picking up the precursors to arktoi magics in infancy. Between that and the fact that arktoi tended to come in a particular flavour of gender, Billie was a rare exception. Not the only exception, not even the only exception in Billie's 'class' but enough of a rarity to be noticed.

Exceptions, like monsters, had no place in the Guild.

Used to living with loving parents and traditional state schooling, Billie had chafed under the expectation, the pressure, and the authority of the Guild training. Their parents had always encouraged questions, encouraged Billie to see things in a nuanced fashion. The Guild liked arktoi to see things in binary categories. Good or bad. Human or monster. Dead or alive.

Billie didn't vibe with binaries.

Still, they were good at their job, the oldest and longest serving arkte in years and one of the youngest to achieve Certified Hunter Status in Guild record. Not that Myles, their handler who signed off every letter with the incredibly impersonal M— the only handwritten piece in the entire sparse page —saw Billie's longevity as a positive. As proven.

This assignment was definitely meant to finish Billie off. But so had the last one. And the one before that.

Acknowledgements

Thank you to my mum for supporting my enjoyment of books and my wanting to tell a thousand stories. Thank you also for not being weird about the smut, not everyone has the capability.

To my in-laws for being my own personal fan club and sneaking peeks every time you visit. The notes you read might not make sense then but I hope they fit in now.

My friends who I stole names from for my high society lot, try to pick yourselves out but I have no intention of confirming or denying anything. Except Stew and James who have a wedding-present character (he's still alive. And not evil. Yay!).

To those who put their writerly knowledge on the internet for people like me to learn from. I wouldn't be here without your generosity.

To my online mutuals, particularly my Tumblr moots: Avra, Sleep, Sparrow & Orion, and more.

And, as always, the pirate queen herself, B. You do incalculable things to make these books possible, if I began to scribble it all down these acknowledgements would get too long for purpose, suffice to say I'm glad we hyphened the surnames so you get a little credit right on the front of every book. Thank you for making me feel like I am, actually, enough just as I am. Even when I'm annoying and won't let you sleep because I have an idea and I want to run it by you.

Thank You So Much For Picking
Up A Copy of
Not The Fainting Kind

For News About My Latest Releases Sign Up
To My Mailing List At:
WillSoulsbyMcCreath.com

Or come find me on Social Media, when I'm
there I'm
@nopoodles

Enjoy my FREE Short Stories over on
nopoodles.wordpress.com

9 781917 179003